She opened her eyes to see him, to confirm that this was him and look at Adan as he kissed her so passionately.

And he was there. Adan was before her with his eyes closed and joy written all over his face.

Twinkling or sparkling behind his right ear caught Zena's eye. She refocused and saw something that looked like fireworks, but then she knew it couldn't be, so she broke the lip-lock from Adan and ordered him to turn around.

"Look! Look!" she screamed, pointing at the shining, clear black night.

As soon as Adan turned, in one second there was a flicker and pop, and two shooting stars raced across the sky.

"Did you see that? Did you see that?" Zena rushed out, still in shock at what she'd just seen.

"Yes! I did! I did! I think it was a shooting star—two shooting stars!" Adan said with his voice half-confused or in awe.

"Oh my God! I can't believe we just saw that!" Zena was ecstatic then and jumping in the sand. She turned to Adan and said with significant cadence, "We just saw that. We just saw that together. Right as we kissed."

Dear Reader,

If we're lucky, our first love is a mirror to self. He or she comes into our lives when we are at our most honest, vulnerable and open. If we're really lucky, like Zena and Adan, that love endures and never leaves us.

Enjoy this intimate narrative of the power of first love and the humble prayer of its return. Escape to the wonder of Bali, Indonesia, with Zena and Adan where they must find their way to a kind of emotional intimacy that promises such an amazing gift of love to us all.

In celebration of love,

Grace O.

Under the Bali Moon

Grace Octavia

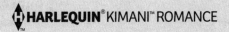
HARLEQUIN® KIMANI™ ROMANCE

Recycling programs
for this product may
not exist in your area.

ISBN-13: 978-0-373-86450-8

Under the Bali Moon

For questions and comments about the quality of this book please contact us
at CustomerService@Harlequin.com.

Printed in U.S.A.

Grace Octavia is a native of Long Island and a graduate of New York University. She also completed her PhD in English at Georgia State University. A proud sister of Delta Sigma Theta Sorority, Incorporated, she is also a member of the Sigma Tau Delta National English Honor Society. The former editor of Rolling Out Urbanstyle Weekly, she lives in Atlanta, GA. She enjoys international travel, hiking, cooking and being with her girlfriends. She currently teaches writing at Spelman College.

Books by Grace Octavia

Harlequin Kimani Romance

Under the Bali Moon

Visit the Author Profile page at
Harlequin.com for more titles.

To my first love, who helped me discover
my first true self and grow boundlessly from there.

Acknowledgments

My dedicated editor, Glenda Howard,
whose help and guidance through this process
was appreciated and invaluable.

Part I

Total Eclipse

Chapter 1

Attorney Zena Nefertiti Shaw looked like a million bucks in the courtroom that afternoon. She was wearing burgundy, thin-heeled suede pumps with matching straps and golden buckles at the ankles that made her feet arch downward with unmistakable femininity. A fitted merlot skirt paired with a dramatic black suit jacket that was gathered in pleats in the small of her back showed off her tiny waist and flat stomach. Her long black hair was pressed and hanging down her back with a subtle curl at the bottom. When Zena moved, her hair floated as if an invisible fan was blowing in her direction for dramatic allure.

In the courtroom in downtown Atlanta, Zena knew she looked good while delivering her closing argument.

"In closing, dear jury, what I want to ask all of you, each of you, is, what would you want if the one you love, the person who stood before man, his family and friends and your family and friends, the church and God in heaven and swore to always love you back, dishonored the innocence of your vows with the unspeakable behaviors Mr. Rayland has imposed upon my client's ever-delicate heart?" Zena posed, releasing the stare that had been locked upon the jury and turning to face Tanisha Rayland, her thirty-seven-year-old client who was at the center of a very ugly and controversial divorce from her bed-hopping R & B husband of twelve years.

Zena stood with her profile parallel to the jury as she gazed at Tanisha. She wanted them to see the connection she had with this woman. Wanted them to see what sympathy for this woman could look like. She folded her arms and exhaled long and deep and dramatically.

"As you all learned throughout these proceedings, and as this woman had to relive, Mrs. Rayland's college sweetheart slept with and impregnated the eighteen-year-old they hired to enter their home to care for their children. And that's only the worst part. *Maybe*. Because in twelve years of marriage, Mrs. Rayland can't recall one year when she wasn't sharing her husband's affections with another woman. Especially not after the fame came to him. Not after the singing career she helped him build took off. After the money started rolling in. Well, then she had to share him with three and four young women at a time."

A tear fell from Tanisha's left eye. She was a woman of striking beauty. Light skin with a red undertone that made her ethnicity unclear until she opened her mouth and the South Side of Chicago came out. Full, pouty lips. Long eyelashes. If it wasn't for the weight she'd put on after having five children—she'd confessed to Zena that she had the last three with hopes of keeping her husband at home and other women away from him—she might look like one of the video vixens with whom Mr. Rayland enjoyed his many indiscretions. And even with the weight, Zena thought Tanisha could easily find work as a full-figured model.

Zena exhaled again, adding hyperbole to Tanisha's tears. She turned back to the jury. As she rolled her eyes along her path, she got a glimpse of Mr. Rayland sitting beside his attorney on the other side of the courtroom. His head was hung low and twisting back and forth in embarrassment or disagreement, as if Zena had shone a light on his deepest, darkest secret. When the divorce proceedings had started, days ago, he'd arrived with

huge diamonds in his ears, a pernicious smile and
a Rolex on his wrist that seemed to connote this
would be a breeze; his wealth would prevail. He
was confident. He stated he would beat the entitlement case. But after days in the courtroom,
he didn't look so sure of this articulation. That
wicked smile was so yesterday. Also gone were
the diamond earrings. That Rolex was a ghost.
He was in his simplest form now. A man without
airs. Humbled.

Eyes on the jury, Zena added, "And the torment
didn't stop with the many affairs. Add in the drugs,
the weeks away from home, the year Mr. Rayland
was in jail and my client had to care for their five
children alone, and the lies." She pursed her lips.
Gave the jury time to recall these infractions she'd
been feeding them over the past few days. Time
to be disgusted with the images of Mr. Rayland
she'd so carefully painted. "The lies. Lie after lie."
She glanced back at Tanisha and her tears. "So, I
ask again, what would you want in return? What
should she want? Can we really place limitations
on what this woman deserves when all she wants
is enough support to care for her children in the
manner to which they've become accustomed, a
return on her investment in her husband and to
stay in the home where she's been living for the
last six years? Respectfully, in contrast with how
Mr. Rayland's attorneys have painted this woman's

request, this isn't about anger or being vindictive or asking for someone to support her. This is about justice. It's about making things right."

Amid grumbles from her opposition, Zena paused and straightened her suit jacket. She leaned against the jury box to appear more vulnerable, as if she was one of them sharing some secret. "Ladies and gentlemen of the jury, I implore you to return to this room with a righteous verdict. To do what's fair. What's just. Award Mrs. Tanisha Rayland twenty-five million dollars in entitlements as she dissolves ties from Mr. Rayland and her sad past with him. Release her, so she can move on. Do what you would want done. What she deserves."

Zena bowed deeply toward the jury, and she actually saw some heads nod back to her. One older woman who'd always smiled at her looked as if she was about to clap. Zena turned back to her seat and winked at her client as she walked toward her. When she sat and grabbed Tanisha's hand beneath the table to reassure her of their success, Zena's assistant and best friend, Malak, who was sitting in the front row, leaned forward smiling.

"This one is in the bag, Z!" Malak cheered in a low voice.

"I hope you're right," Zena whispered, eyeing Mr. Rayland's attorney, who was standing before the jury, ready to present his closing arguments before the jury would return to their room to vote.

Zena really did need to have this one in the bag. When Tanisha left her husband, he froze all of her accounts and she had little money to cover Zena's high hourly fee. Since news of the Raylands' pending divorce broke, the hungry media made a gossip sensation of Tanisha's life and split from the R & B crooner many saw as a stable and loving husband—at least that's how his team had been portraying him in all the gossip rags. Zena had to play offense and defense, creating a team for her client, which now included her firm's personal publicist, security staff member and photographer. This robbed her other cases of valuable time—and her bank account of precious dollars. Zena told herself this was the cost of maintaining her firm's reputation. All of this while praying a big payday would come when, as Malak predicted, "this one is in the bag."

"Don't worry," Zena said to Tanisha, but it was clear she was also trying to encourage herself. "Everything will be fine."

Luckily, Malak's psychic sensibilities were better than her jet-black-and-blond ombré weave.

After just twenty minutes of deliberating, the jury returned with a verdict that made a rich woman of Zena's client. She'd be able to pay Zena's fees and those of her associates and, more importantly, move on with her life.

Moving on for Zena, though, meant her usual posttrial trip to Margarita Town with Malak in tow. After debriefing Tanisha on their next steps and assuring her this was "really it—she'd won," Zena hopped into a Town Car waiting outside the courthouse and quietly thanked God for the magical mix of tequila and strawberry flavoring awaiting her arrival at Margarita Town. It would wash away all of her thoughts of Mr. Priest Rayland and his deplorable behavior.

"You shut that fool all the way down," Malak said later, sitting across from Zena at Margarita Town. Before her was a behemoth of a margarita glass, the size of a baby's head, filled to the rim with frothy blue ice chips and liquid. "I thought he was going to hop out of his chair and run across the room to start choking you at any moment." Malak laughed and held her hands up as if she had them wrapped around Zena's neck.

Behind her was the normal fare of a margarita bar. Nothing fancy. Nothing too nice. Soft red lights set aglow garage-sale rainbow ponchos, sombreros and dusty, half-clothed Lupita dolls tacked to the walls. No one was there for the decor, though. It was just a theme for the real prize that attracted professionals to Margarita Town's lopsided high-top tables and sticky bar each night after work. The clientele included burned-out teachers, lawyers, doctors, publicists, business owners, even yoga teachers.

The red ice in Zena's significantly smaller margarita glass was nearly gone, and Zena was already feeling the soothing affects of the concoction, so she laughed more deeply than Malak had expected.

"Slow down, cowgirl," Malak teased. "You know you're a lightweight. I don't want to carry you out of here."

Malak and Zena had been best friends since high school. They were nothing alike, but since the first day they met when Zena had moved to Atlanta, Georgia, from Queens, New York, and chose a seat behind Malak in her first-period history class, they were together through most of life's laughs and hard times. That was why when Zena finished law school at Howard and returned to Atlanta to start her own practice, she called Malak, who only finished high school with a GED, and offered Malak a job as her assistant. Zena trusted Malak, and as a new attorney building a practice in the ever-cliquish legal field, she wanted someone by her side who would anticipate her moves, encourage her and keep her laughing. Malak was good at all of those things, but what made her most valuable to Zena, what she knew when she hired Malak, was that she was whip smart. While she'd made some poor choices, including getting pregnant by her boyfriend senior year of high school,

Malak was smarter than many of the cohorts Zena went up against during mock trials in law school. While Zena always made it a point to check in on her old friend and encourage her to go back to school, Malak wanted to try to make her family work and got married right out of high school. By the time she was twenty-five, she was divorced with two children. Zena vowed to return home to make sure Malak had a chance to really turn things around.

"No slowing down for me tonight. Actually, I think I'll have another," Zena said, signaling for the waitress to bring a second margarita. "I need to wash the memory of that sneaky, slithering snake out of my mind. We have new blood in the morning, and I don't want to stay up all night thinking about—" She stopped and looked off, forlorn.

"I know what you mean," Malak agreed pensively, flipping ombré tendrils over her shoulder. "He really did a number on her. A number on you, too."

"Me?" Zena smiled as if Malak had to be joking. "How did he do a number on me?"

"Um…" Malak nodded to the new margarita the waitress was sliding on the table before Zena.

Zena was no drinker. While she always indulged a little after they'd closed a case, too much alcohol almost always made her a bit emotional.

"Come on. I'm just celebrating. Of course, I

hated that toad, but it's not like I took anything he did personally. It's not like he did that mess to me."

"I couldn't tell," Malak pointed out. "Not the way you were carrying on these last few days— hell, since the case began. It was like you *had* to win. You had to beat him."

"Isn't that common? Why I have an unblemished record in the courtroom?" Zena's tone was snarky. Overly confident. But still comical. While she was just thirty-one, after six years in the courtroom as the sole attorney at Z. Shaw Law, she made a name for herself as a fearless and swift attorney. One of her first cases was a long shot. Her sorority sister from Bethune-Cookman had married a football pro who was smart enough to lock her into an ironclad prenup before making her his punching bag. The football wife came to Zena with no money and no way out of the dysfunctional marriage. While Zena had little experience and could barely pay her bills, she took on the case pro bono. There was something about the messy marriage that turned a knife in Zena's gut, and she spent day and night on the case. In the end, she found a loophole in the prenup and won a nice settlement for her client.

Of course, the case took over news headlines for weeks, making young Zena a new name to know in legal circles. Quickly, Z. Shaw became one of a few top firms in the city that represented high-profile clients in divorce cases involving entitlement hearings where large sums of money were on the table. Ninety-nine percent of her clients were women seeking settlements from their cheating and very wealthy husbands. These were cases with obvious winners and losers. Bad boys who'd done good girls wrong. Zena knew the right buttons to push in the courtroom. She always got her ruling.

Zena's cell phone started rattling beside her margarita on the table. She looked down. Zola was on the screen.

"Oh, man, I don't even feel like talking to her right now," Zena said, letting the phone vibrate. "You know she only calls if she needs money—or to borrow something."

"Maybe you should answer. She's been calling all day," Malak said.

"All day?" Zena repeated, surprised and staring at Malak as if she'd somehow failed as an assistant. "Why didn't you tell me?"

Zena moved to answer the phone, but the ringing had already stopped and was replaced with the clatter of an incoming text message:

ZOLA: Z, call me back. I've been calling you all day. I have news.

Zena looked at the screen and repeated "news"

aloud. "What the hell?" she added. "What kind of news could she have?"

Malak looked away nervously, but Zena didn't question her because she was busy getting up from her seat to return Zola's call.

"I'll be right back," Zena said, already out of the booth across from Malak. "Don't let anyone spike my drink."

"Sure won't, Boss Lady," Malak confirmed solidly.

The friends laughed, and Zena made her way through the joyous, drunken crowd of now-smiling professionals. Zena recognized a guy she'd met on a dating website standing by the bar with a beer in his hand. His white business shirt was unbuttoned to his chest; opposing ends of an open tie flanked each shoulder. Men and women who looked as if they must be his colleagues stood laughing at something he'd just said. When he saw Zena, he waved, but she turned her head, pressed her cold cell phone to her ear to pretend to be on a call and padded quickly toward the door.

Outside Margartia Town, Zena found a place on the curb beside a skinny and stylish East Indian couple smoking cigarettes and dialed Zola's number. Beneath the amber glow of an oversize blow-up margarita glass filled with plastic golden liquid, she pressed the phone to her ear again, crossed her arms and rolled her eyes at the couple in heightened disgust at their activity. While the early-summer afternoon heat had cleared with the sunset, it was still too hot and muggy outside in Georgia to withstand the stale, dry air of cigarette smoke. Just when Zena was about to mention the local ordinance banning smoking in the private dining zone, Zola answered.

"Zeeeennnaaaa!" Zola squealed into the phone so loudly Zena winced and pulled the receiver back from her ear. There was a brazen exuberance and cheeriness to Zola's voice. She sounded like a pre-game high school cheerleader, eager and enthusiastic, but decidedly so. Determinedly so. The voice was simply the calling card of everything else about the little sister on the other end of the phone. She was the metaphor of a smile. Anxiously happy. Not only was her glass always half-full, but it also filled with sugary pink lemonade and she was all too excited to share with everyone else. But that was how she'd decided to be; how Zola made herself function.

As the sisters exchanged common salutations filled with updates and weather predictions, Zena relaxed in the comfort of her sister's arbitrary joyfulness. There was always something about the sweet spirit in Zola that calmed and loosened the uptight and upright spirit in Zena.

"I was actually surprised we won," Zena acknowledged on the tail end of a summary about her adventure in the courtroom closing Priest Rayland's case. "Of course, we had enough evidence stacked against that fool to make it impossible for the jury to rule in his favor, but you just never know these days. I used to expect the jury to rule based upon facts, but it's really all emotion. All feeling. You'll see." Zena inhaled deeply as the couple departed after taking their final puffs. "Enough about me. What's up with you? How's studying going for my future partner?" Zena's voice was wrapped in giddiness then.

Just two weeks ago, Zena was in Washington, DC, for Zola's law school graduation at Howard. Though Zola originally planned to move to New York City to pursue her dream of being a fashion critic after undergrad, with much prodding and planning and some strings pulled by Zena, Zola attended her big sister's law school alma mater, graduated with decent marks, and now it was just a matter of getting Zola to pass the Georgia Bar Exam before she'd be the newest addition to Z. Shaw Law, soon to be Z. and Z. Shaw Law.

"Um…it's going fine," Zola let out with a marked zip in her zeal. "Okay, I guess… It's cool—"

Zena cut in, ready to inspire, ready to employ the swift hand of big sister judgment that had already decided that Zola wasn't living up to her potential. She needed to let Zola know this slacking was dangerous. She needed to inspire Zola to do better. And this was the way things had always been between the sisters.

"You don't sound like it's 'cool.' Come on, Zola. Don't drop the ball now. You can do this. I'm paying your bills, so you don't have to work. All you have to do every day is study. You know how many people wish they had that privilege? I know I did."

Sounding diminished, Zola started, "I know. I know—but—"

Zena cut her off again, though. "Look, you're smart. You can do this. You have to focus. Focus and don't accept mediocrity. I keep telling you that."

"I know I *can* do it, Zena, but that's what I'm calling to talk to you about—I don't think I *want* to do it right now."

"What? What do you mean 'want'?" Zena's face contorted into something that looked like an angered question mark. She looked at the phone as if Zola could see her cold stare. As she had all of those times in the past, Zena felt she just needed to find the right words of encouragement to entice Zola to change her view. Should she be stern or sensitive? What would work best at such a crossroads just shy of eight weeks before the July Georgia Bar Exam?

"This isn't about your clock, Zola. It's not about whether now is the time for you. Now is the only time. You have to take the Bar. You have to take it this summer."

There was silence then—the kind that signifies that there's more information coming.

"Wait, didn't your text say you had news?" Zena recalled. "Is that what this is about? What's going on?" Images depicting a reel of disaster rolled through Zena's mind—Zola had already run off to New York to dance in hip-hop music videos; she'd used all the money Zena had been giving her for rent to pay for a secret drug habit; she hadn't even started studying; she was preg— "Are you preg—?"

Zola stopped her sister's stream of dark thoughts with a soft and mousy revelation: "Alton asked me to elope. That's what I've been trying to get out. That's why I've been calling you all day. We decided to just do it—to just get married. Now." Zola was referring to her recent status as the fiancée of Alton Douglass, her childhood sweetheart and long-term boyfriend, who'd just popped the question at Zola's graduation in DC. While Zena wasn't exactly hip to the idea of Alton and Zola getting married right when Zola was about to really start her career, as she watched her baby sister cry when Alton slid the stoneless silver ring he'd called "antique" onto Zola's finger, Zena was reconciled knowing that it would be at least one year before there was even a discussion about a wedding. By then, Zola would be back in Atlanta, have passed the Bar Exam and be a practicing attorney.

"Zena? Zena? You there?" Zola called after a long pause.

"Yes. I am." Zena's words were void of emotion but somehow also overly laden with something else.

"So?" Zola paused awkwardly. "What do you think? No big wedding. We're just going to do it. Get married and start living our lives. It's a smart decision—right?"

Though there was the common glee in Zola's tone, there was a stiffness there now, too—a covering used to veil her joy in some way. To protect it.

Zena could sense all of this.

Zena began pacing in small circles, subconsciously reaffirming the existence of her environment as she prepared to quiz Zola. She felt as if she was being sucked away. As if the smoking couple had returned and lit up new cigarettes to steal her air.

She looked back up at the oversize plastic margarita glass hovering over her. It was glowy and amber. Happy. This was her happy place.

She wished Malak was outside Margarita Town standing beside her to hear this. She'd put Zola on speaker and have her best friend there to share her disbelief, confirm this horrible mistake Zola was about to make. A mistake Zena would have to clean up. The thing was, Zena had been protecting her baby sister for so long, there was no way she would let anything like that happen. She loved Zola so much, and she'd gotten her so far. They were almost there—almost at the finish line.

"Well did you tell Mommy and Daddy? What did they say about this?" Zena asked.

"Daddy's too busy with whatever up in New York. And Mommy loves Alton, of course. Who doesn't love Alton?" The adoration in Zola's voice was so absolute Zena imagined that Alton must be standing right beside her, listening in and probably laughing at Zena's reaction. Maybe *Zena* was the one on speakerphone.

"Of course everyone loves Alton," Zena said with years of knowing and, yes, loving sweet and kind Alton, Zola's spiritual twin, laced in her words. While Zena, at fifteen, was nearly in love with the mere vision of Alton's older brother, Adan, Alton was actually like a little brother to Zena.

"All of this seems so sudden. Like, who's going to pay for all of this?"

"Really, Z? I can't believe you asked me that. I say I'm getting married and you ask who's paying?"

"It's a perfectly reasonable question. I've been supporting you, and Alton isn't exactly rolling in the dough."

"He's a singer. That's just how it goes when you're just starting out. But he is getting money for his songwriting. And he's about to sign a deal with a major label. We just have to hold out."

"Sure, 'hold out,'" Zena shot nastily, though she hadn't intended on sounding so awful.

"Z, I knew you wouldn't take this well— especially since I'm supposed to be preparing and everything. But I at least thought you'd be excited. Like happy for me," Zola said.

"I am happy for you. It's just—" Zena paused and looked at the inflated margarita glass again for inspiration. She needed to say the right thing, find the right words. She needed to support her sister. Be there for her sister. But how could she do that if she felt her sister was doing the wrong thing? Marriage? It wasn't the right time. How could she support that? Be there for that? Didn't support and being "there" for her sister mean telling the truth? Telling it like it is? Zena looked away from the margarita glass and let go of the idea of saying the right thing. She decided to say exactly what was on her mind. "What about your life… your future?" Zena let out, and she immediately hated every word she'd said. She sounded like their mother, like their grandmother.

"My *future*?" Zola laughed at this assertion in a way that Zena hated. The statement and tone reeked of "my big sister is crazy and cold. She doesn't get it." Zola took to using the tone whenever Zena said something with which Zola found fault or could easily deconstruct. "Z, listen, Alton is my future. Not being an attorney. That's just a job. I know how you feel about it—it's your life—but that's not how I see it."

Zola's last sentence grated against something in Zena.

"Don't do that. Don't go there." Suddenly, Zena felt incredibly lonely standing out there in front of Margarita Town. Cold. Bare. Though no breeze had passed, she shuddered and turned to peek through the front window of Margarita Town to find Malak's face. "I'm just trying to look out for you. You know? That's all I'm doing. That's all I've ever done."

"I know. And I love you for it. And I'm still taking the Bar Exam. Just not this year."

"What? Why not? It's scheduled for July—that's like eight weeks from now. You've been studying, right?"

"Well, that's kind of the other thing I wanted to tell you."

"What?"

"Alton is so excited about this whole thing—well, we both are—anyway, he really wants to do it right away. And I agree with him—I love him and I want to be his wife—sooner rather than later, of course," Zola clattered out as if she was explaining this all to herself. "He wants to elope—now."

Again, Zena felt herself drifting away. What was happening?

"So, we're getting married in two weeks," Zola went on, ignoring her sister's silence.

"Two? Two weeks? I thought you meant like six months—three at the very least. How are you going to get married in two weeks? And where are you going to get married in two weeks? That's like impossible. Any decent place has a waiting list of like nine months. And please don't tell me you two are going to the Justice of the Peace. And not Vegas!" Zena felt herself growing more aggravated, so she paused for a second before beginning again with less sharpness in her tone. "Listen, Zol, why are you doing this? Is there something you need to tell me? Are you pregnant?"

"I can't believe you just suggested that, but I already told you that I'm not pregnant. I'm just in love. And I'm not getting married in Vegas or at the courthouse. We're going to do it in Bali. We're getting married in Bali."

Zena could hear the smile return to Zola's face as she went on revealing her plan. The wedding would be a small seaside ceremony. No audience. Only two witnesses in attendance. Zola wanted Zena to be there as her maid of honor. The second witness would be the best man: Alton's older brother; Zena's old flame… Adan.

After more minutes of sibling emotional wrangling in the form of probing questions and slick statements, Zola was back in Margarita Town sitting across from Malak.

"You knew? You knew? All this time, you knew they were eloping and you didn't tell me?" Zena had shifted her interrogation to Malak, who sat there buzzing from her second big blue margarita and holding her hands in the air innocently.

"She just told me a few hours ago. Right before we went into the courtroom," she said. "I didn't exactly want to tell you before you were walking in to give your closing."

"But what about after? Why didn't you tell me after? Immediately after?"

"Because I wanted Zola to tell you herself. I wanted it to be a surprise. And don't you think you're kind of missing the point here? The point is that your little sister is getting married? It's great news. Right?" Malak smiled, though she knew the expression would not be returned.

"Not exactly. This is a big mistake for her right now. They aren't ready to get married. Yes, they're in love. But they don't have enough money. They're just banking on Alton getting this record deal. This is a recipe for disaster and you know it.

We're in the business of watching marriages fail. And what makes most marriages fail?"

"Money," Malak reluctantly mumbled.

"Exactly. When money is short, people start changing. They become horrible versions of themselves. And I'm not saying they'll always be poor. I'm not going to wish doom on Alton's career or anything, but being a performer has its ups and downs."

"Alton and Zola have been together forever. They'll be okay."

"They have no idea what they're in for. What's going to happen to them," Zola said to herself as if she hadn't heard anything Malak said. "I just can't sit back and watch Zola do this—mess everything up that we've worked so hard for."

Malak's best attempts to placate her friend turned to annoyance. "Why do you do that to Zola? Always act like she has no clue? Like she's stupid and can't make any decisions without you?" Malak paused and looked down into her drink. She exhaled and grimaced frankly, as if she was about to say something she might regret. "You know, maybe this isn't about the wedding—about Alton and Zena getting engaged. Maybe your reaction is about—you know—*him*. And the fact that he is going to be there in Bali."

Him and *he* needed no further explanation. The words bounced from Malak's mouth like a fireball and landed on the table before Zena. She wanted to pick it up and throw it across the room, get it away from her as soon as possible, but she was also afraid to touch it, afraid to hear it, to think it, to think of *him*.

"Don't bring *him* up," Zena scoffed, and she sounded like a little girl.

"I have to. Sorry, Z. But there's no way you haven't thought about him. His brother is marrying your little sister. That has to matter. Right? Everyone thought you guys would do it first. And now Zola and Alton are getting married and you two will be together for that. It's been so long. When was the last time you spoke to Ad—"

"Don't say his name," Zena cut in. "I don't want to hear it. And I don't want to talk about it. And I don't care about him. And I don't think about him. My opinion of this disaster of a wedding that's about to take place in two freaking weeks has nothing to do with Adan—" Zena tried to stop her diatribe before she got to the name that was flashing in her head, but out it came.

Malak was right. Zena had thought of Adan, of course. And while she'd done a grand but strategic job of avoiding him and all topics concerning him, when Alton proposed to Zola in DC, Zena knew she'd finally have to see Adan. But then she figured she had at least a year—one year to get her head together. She could even meet a wonderful, well-traveled, well-read man, who was also funny and down-to-earth and rich, and get married—at least engaged—okay, at least committed. She'd arrive at Zola and Alton's wedding to see Adan and his NYC doctor wife and perfect children, and Zena would have to show for her own life a successful law practice, bombshell body and hot judge husband, with dimples—fiancé—okay, boyfriend. But now everything had changed.

"Okay. I won't make you talk about Adan. If you say you haven't thought of him and you don't want to think of him, then we can move on to something else," Malak agreed patronizingly, as if she was some kind of barroom therapist. "We can focus on what's really important. And that's Zola's happiness. That girl loves you. She trusts you. She adores you. She admires you. She needs your support. Can you just support her?"

"I'll support the right decision. That's what I'll support." Zena rolled her eyes and waved to a random waitress who was rushing past their table. She asked her, "Can you have our waitress get our check?"

"No problem, hon," the woman said, sounding more cheerful than she actually looked. "I'll actually just get it for you."

"Thanks," Zena said as the thought of seeing Adan again suddenly hit her. After so many years of blocking painful memories, she wondered if her heart was strong enough to deal with his actual presence. Zena quietly considered that maybe they would be distant, even mockingly cordial. She'd feel like she was meeting a stranger, a stranger who maybe just happened to look like someone she knew. Someone she'd known for a very long time. But Adan was no stranger. He was once Zena's everything. He was her past, what she'd hoped would become her future. But that was all gone now. And it was all because of him.

Chapter 2

The morning after drowning the news of Zola's pending Bali wedding in the murky brown liquid of so many shots of reposado tequila she could hardly leave Margarita Town on her feet, Zena awoke to a spinning headache that released her from her morning run. She rolled over in the bed, turning her back to the bedroom window where the late-morning sun was beaming into the room. She was too tired to be fully awake and ready to enter a new day after tossing around in bed through the twilight hours, endlessly replaying worries she had no control over. Problems she'd trained herself to forget, to get away from, but now, there they were right in front of her. While her nighttime thoughts began with Zola, the prickling concern beneath her sister's future was Zena's own past.

Malak's psychic ability—or good sense—had struck gold again at Margarita Town when she boldly shared that maybe much of Zena's consternation about Alton and Zola getting married wasn't about them finding love. It was about the love Zena had lost and never forgotten.

Zola wasn't the only sister to fall in love with a boy who lived up the street. She actually wasn't even the first.

Lying in bed that night, Zena's thoughts went back—way back to the time she was a teenager and met Adan Frederick Douglass. He was the first boy to steal her heart away. He was the first man to tear her heart into tiny smithereens. She'd spent too much of her life and good money in therapy trying to pull the pieces back together.

It all started with her parents' ruined marriage and a popped bicycle chain.

After her father's second affair with one of the cashiers at the Sutphin Boulevard Burger King where he was a manager, Zena's mother paid a few hundred to a pimply-faced attorney who promised "quick" divorces in advertisements on subway cars. The couple had no money, property or belongings to split up. Her mother knew there was no way her husband would petition the courts for custody or shared visitation rights for Zena and Zola, fifteen and nine at the time—he had limited funds and no place for his daughters to stay. Zena overheard her mother telling their neighbor who worked on Jamaica Avenue that she just wanted the marriage to be over and to get her girls out of Queens.

Hearing this hurt Zena beyond repair. While her parents' marriage was mostly rocky, as her father was unreliable and could never keep a long-term job to support them and often stepped out on her mother, Zena loved her father and just wished he'd do right. During their father-daughter walks around the neighborhood, he'd often promise just that. He explained that he didn't mean to hurt her mother and said something about New York's poor public school system that diagnosed his dyslexia too late. His reasoning became scrambled into a massive puzzle in Zena's head. All she wanted to hear about was how her parents and her family could stay together. But he had no solutions. No plans. "I'm broken, babygirl. I done failed ya'll," he'd said.

A week later, Zena was standing in a Greyhound bus line with her mother and sister at the Port Authority Bus Terminal in Manhattan. Everything they owned amounted to five boxes being slid into the cargo hold of a bus en route to Atlanta, Georgia. Speaking as if she was a grown woman who'd lived a life and had the necessary scars on her soul one would need to give another grown woman advice, Zena said in her gruff Jamaica, Queens-girl accent, "You didn't even give him a chance. He was trying and you didn't give him a chance. And I resent you for that." Zena thought she'd really said something. Standing in line at the Port Authority Bus Terminal, she crossed her slender teenage arms over her chest and awaited a defense she felt was impossible.

"Mothers don't have time to give people chances. You're my top priority. Not him. Not even me. I did this to save you and your sister from growing up and being stuck in a hole like me and your daddy. I did this so you could be happy," her mother said.

"Happy? In Georgia?" Zena laughed the way any Queens-born girl who'd been torn from her home to live in Georgia would. "You're making us move from our friends and school. We're losing everything, Mommy."

Zena's mother paused and responded with unmistakable passion in her voice. "You may feel like that now, but I'm giving you a real opportunity to have a better life."

* * *

Zena's bicycle chain had popped the morning she met Adan. Her mother had just gotten the rickety red ten-speed from the Salvation Army and unloaded it from the back of the dented 4Runner some cross-eyed deacon at their new church let her mother borrow. Zena was complaining about being locked up all day in the house looking after Zola and begged for a bicycle. While she'd complained about cobwebs on the frame and the cracking fake-leather seat when they spotted the ten-speed in the back of the secondhand store, once Zena got the thing home and kicked off from the curb, she tasted the kind of freedom every fifteen-year-old knew while riding a bicycle.

At first, she heeded her mother's instructions and only rode around the corner a few times, but then she became curious about her new surroundings and rode faster, standing up on the pedals as she pushed two and three miles from her front door. The houses got bigger and the cars nicer as she sped along. She noticed that the house she lived in with her mother and her sister was the smallest one in the entire neighborhood. She'd heard her mother mention on the phone to her grandmother that she'd gotten the rental for a quarter of the price through some pilot fair-housing project that would later be known as "Section 8 housing."

It was late summer, and the Georgia heat kept

most people indoors, but she saw some stray gag-
gles of teenagers entering cars and front doors and
wondered if any of them would be her classmates
when she started classes at her new high school in
a few weeks. Walking up flower-lined driveways
in bright colors and smiling, they all looked so solidly middle-class, so happy, so far away from the
armor-clad, stone-faced friends she knew back in
the New York projects. Right then, Zena decided
that she wasn't going to tell anyone at her new
school that she lived in the smallest house in the
neighborhood.

Soon, droplets of warm sweat escaped Zena's
underarms and wet her T-shirt. The precipitation
seemed to descend on her brow and draw every
ounce of energy from her body. Zena, going on
pure zeal, continued her tour, but she was pant-
ing like a thirsty dog and she began feeling as if
she'd been away from home for hours, though it
had only been twenty minutes since her departure.
This was her official introduction to the stifling
Georgia humidity that suffocated everything that
had the nerve to move before 7 p.m. in late July.
Zena would never forget that feeling, that day; it
was as if she'd fallen asleep in a sauna and awoke
in a pool of her own sweat.

Growing concerned after considering her wet
knuckles and steamy scalp, Zena decided to head

home, fearing her mother must be panicked because she'd been gone so long.

She'd been resting her bottom on the prickly cracked bicycle seat but decided to get up and floor it home.

When she rounded the curb onto her new street, catching a breeze that did little to cool her off, Zena noticed a family getting out of their car in the driveway on the side of a house that looked identical to the one she lived in just seven houses down. It was a mother and father with two boys. One of the boys looked her age. The other couldn't be much older than Zola.

While Zena was two houses away, the family stopped and looked at her as if she was an alien pushing a ten-speed up the street.

Zena's delicate fifteen-year-old self-esteem made her wonder if she was doing something wrong. Could they see the sweat stains at her underarms? Had the wind swept her hair all over her head and she looked like a parading Medusa? What were they looking at?

The little boy started waving, but Zena was too afraid to wave back, fearing she'd lose control of her bike and crash into one of the cars parked on the street. Instead, her bubbling anxiety under their watching eyes made her want to simply disappear, so Zena decided to race home, where she'd run into the house and never ever emerge again.

That was when the chain popped.

The pedal push that was supposed to send her somewhere quickly actually split the chain. There was a click and then the bike simply stopped moving. Zena's insistence on continuing her pedaling sent her and the bike, rather quickly and very dramatically, to the hot tar pavement, where she really hoped she would die.

"Lord, she done fainted," Zena heard a man's voice say, so she knew she hadn't actually died, which was a letdown.

"No, she didn't. I think she just fell," she heard a woman's voice say, and she knew it was the mother, who'd been standing by the car, because as she looked up from the ground, she could see the woman's coral espadrilles rushing toward her.

Soon, the family of four was gathered around Zena as if she was a fallen angel. Worry was on everyone's face. Everyone but the boy who looked her age. He was smiling. Almost laughing at the sight.

Zena was quiet, quieter than she'd ever been in life. She watched as the four fussed over her, trying to figure out what had gone wrong. The father discovered that it was the broken chain that sent her tumbling to the ground, but he kept saying something about the heat and that it was too hot for anyone to be riding a bicycle at 3 p.m. And didn't she know that? The mother tried to quiet him after sending the little boy into the house for water.

She asked, "Where are your parents, honey? You live around here?" Her voice was Southern sweet. She sounded as if she could get anything from anyone. Zena had never heard a woman sound quite like that. It made her instantly like the woman.

Zena was listening but not speaking so the mother made the father check for broken bones. He found none and announced that Zena was just in shock. Just afraid because she'd fallen from her bike and here they were hawking over her like police officers. The couple laughed in unison at their hovering in a way that Zena had never heard her parents connect. It was as if they were suddenly alone and had heard lines in a conversation no one else could hear. Then the father kissed the mother. He said, "That's the nurse in my baby. Always worried about somebody." They kissed again and giggled.

The boy who was about Zena's age, the one who'd been ready to laugh at her fall, was frowning then and rolling his eyes at his parents as if he'd seen this all before and it was making him sick. He turned to Zena and pointed his index finger into his open mouth toward his tonsils as if he was about to make himself vomit.

The little comical gesture introduced Zena to

the saying, "I have butterflies in my stomach," because some new feeling was literally tickling her insides, from her navel to her throat. At that very moment, the tough girl from Queens awakened into feelings she'd never known. It was as if those little butterflies fluttered their delicate wings at her insides all at once and sent some mellifluous whispers of what she'd later recognize as first love straight to her heart. She'd never even thought of looking at a boy the way she did at that moment. She wanted to know everything about him. To smell him. To touch his curly black hair. Kiss those full lips. And if she'd ever heard the word *imbibe*, she'd want that—to imbibe him. Drink him in. Soak him up. Absorb him so she could feel what she was feeling in her stomach again and again. But that would come later. Junior year in high school. In someone's basement after a football game. Right then, she just wanted to know one thing—his name.

And without Zena even asking, he acquiesced.

"I'm Adan," he said, struggling so hard to make his pubescent voice sound masculine as his parents came out of their love bubble and noticed the teenagers' quick connection.

"I'm Zena," was returned.

"She speaks," the father said, looking at the mother with a kind of adult knowing in his voice.

"Good to hear, honey," the mother said. "We're

the Douglasses. You've met Adan already. This is Mr. Roy." She pointed to the father and then to herself. "I'm Mrs. Pam. And that little hellion who never came out with the water is Adan's little brother, Alton. He's probably playing his Nintendo game."

After helping Zena to her feet and carrying her bicycle to the sidewalk as she reluctantly revealed that she lived up the street and had just moved to Georgia from New York with her mother and sister, Roy abruptly excused himself and his wife. Attempting to pull Pam toward the house, he winked at Adan and ordered him to fix the chain with the supplies in the garage. Pam ignored Roy's clear desire that Adan and Zena get better acquainted and asked about Zena's mother again. She wanted to make sure Zena got home okay.

"The girl just told you she lives up the street. I think they're renting the Jefferson's old house. That ain't far. She'll be fine, Pam!" Roy protested. "Let these young folks figure it out. Everything will work out fine." He winked at Adan again and pulled his wife up the walkway and into the house.

"They're so weird. Weird and embarrassing," Adan said when they were gone, and with every word he spoke, Zena felt those wondrous flutters all through her body again.

"My parents are divorced," Zena announced as if she'd been holding it in her stomach all that time and needed to let someone know. "My dad cheated. He's having a baby."

Adan hardly reacted. He just shrugged in his learned teenage boy way. Zena would soon recognize this as his cool routine. "My mom would kill my dad if he cheated. She told him that one night. I think he believes her."

Adan picked up the bicycle and began rolling it toward the garage.

Zena followed close behind, watching him walk, spying his muscular arms and calves. She kept thinking that he had to be the cutest boy she'd ever seen. But, then, she couldn't remember ever really seeing any other boys. Memories of the ones who'd chased her around her neighborhood in Queens had faded so quickly. Who were they? What were their names again?

"Your chain is mad rusty. Where'd you get this bike? The Salvation Army?" he asked jokingly once they were in the garage and out of the hot sun.

"Yes," Zena admitted, embarrassed, and then she wished she hadn't fessed up to it. She didn't want Adan to know she was poor. Then he wouldn't like her. Could he like her? Did he? Zena looked into Adan's eyes for signs of something. Anything.

"Really?" Adan seemed surprised by the news and the obvious fumble of his joke about the Salvation Army. His light brown cheeks turned ruddy, and suddenly Zena saw in his eyes reflections of the same feelings she felt in her stomach. He liked her. Maybe he did. She felt her own cheeks turning red then.

"That's cool anyway. The bike is a little rusty. It could use some cleaning. But it's a nice bike. A Huffy," Adan said, suddenly cutting his gaze away from Zena as if he was becoming more nervous.

"You think it's nice?"

"Yes. It is. I could help you fix it up if you like. We could spray paint it. Make it dope." Adan looked back at Zena and smiled.

Zena smiled back. She felt as if she'd been asked out on her first date. "That would be cool," she said.

"We could set it up here in the garage. Work on it. Like a project."

Zena had never heard a boy her age use that word before—*project*.

She nodded and helped Adan flip the bike over. Standing beside him, she didn't want to breathe. She didn't want a second more to pass. She wanted everything to stop so she could just be right there, right then with him. She was afraid she'd miss something. Forget something about that moment. But she never would.

He turned on an old, dusty radio that his father listened to sometimes when he worked on his car in the garage. Some Goodie Mob song was playing, and Zena revealed that she'd never heard of the group. Adan's eyes widened. He didn't believe her. He then went through the entire history of the Dungeon Family, a local rap consortium that Adan heralded as the best MCs in the world. Zena laughed and pointed out that the best MCs were Biggie, Nas and Jay Z. This debate would continue throughout their relationship. But at that moment, Adan controlled the dial on the radio, so he turned up Goodie Mob's "Black Ice." Loud and proud, he rapped along about waking up and touching the sky.

Zena watched, listened and laughed. Soon, just as she'd done with the boys back in NYC, she forgot all about the time. The sun went down and her mother came looking for her.

It took Adan three long, hot weeks to make Zena's old rusty bike the envy of the street. With his father's help, he spray painted the Huffy hot pink and electric blue, reupholstered the seat with purple fabric and Pam even added a bell that Zena's mother insisted on paying for. As the repairs went on and the summer came to a close, Zena learned more about the Douglasses and everything about Adan. He was so smart. He seemed so much older than her. Sometimes he reminded her of Mr. Roy in the way he was always joking and pretending he was keen on a secret. He was cool, too. Seldom overexcited or sad. He seemed to have feelings right down the middle at all times. He took care of his little brother. Listened to his mother. Followed his father's direction. This all comforted Zena. Made her open up to Adan about everything that had her out pedaling fast on that old red bike that day. Over those afternoons in the garage she told him all about her parents' divorce. Her empty feelings. Her fear. He always seemed to know just what to say. Just when to be silent. Just when to reach out to wipe her tears.

One evening, Zena's mother had to work a double shift at the airport, where she'd lucked up on a job at Delta Air Lines. Zena was stuck in the house taking care of Zola, though she'd promised Adan she'd meet him at the local roller-skating rink. She was too embarrassed to call his house to say why she couldn't go, so she decided to just let the moment pass and later lie and say she forgot. While this line of thinking sounded crazy to her now, back then, it was a perfectly rational decision made out of shame and humiliation that her family had such limited funds that she was basically her sister's primary caretaker while her mother plated flight meals at the airport. Zena had been spending so much time at the Douglasses, and she now envied the ease and reliability of Mr. Roy and Mrs. Pam's stable marriage and home. Adan never had to take care of Alton. There was always someone at home to look after them.

After watching too many music videos on BET, Zena told Zola that it was time to get ready for bed and ordered her little sister to go take a shower. Once Zola finished complaining about the shower and begged to watch more videos, Zena scolded her as if she was the mother, and Zola stomped out of the living room toward the bathroom.

"I don't hear the water," Zena hollered after a while, and then the sound of the water in the shower finally started. She reminded herself to bust into the bathroom in a few minutes to make sure Zola was really in the shower and not just looking at the water—her mother always did that.

Zena got up to turn off the television and there was a faint, soft knock at the front door.

On instinct, Zena looked around the room for her father's baseball bat, but then reminded herself that she was no longer in the projects and that bat was still in New York.

"Who is it?" Zena demanded forcefully, trying to make her voice sound louder, gruffer in case there was a dangerous criminal at the door.

"Adan."

An alarm sounded in Zena's heart. She was quickly frantic. Why was Adan at her front door? He'd been past her house. He'd walked her home on some nights when she'd been at his house until it was too dark for her to walk home alone. But he'd never rung the front door. He'd certainly never been inside. Did he want to come inside? Everything around Zena seemed to be in complete disarray. Messy. Too messy. Zola's stupid Oreo crumbs on the secondhand couch. Their dirty sneakers lined up beside the front door. Her mother's work clothes on the chair. Zena looked into the dining room. They didn't even have a set in there yet. No chairs. No table. Just a bright light and an empty room.

"Zena?" Adan called from outside as if he sensed that he'd been forgotten.

"Yes."

"You going to open the door?"

Zena exhaled and walked to the entrance, where she forced a casual smile before opening the door only a few inches.

Adan was standing on the steps with his hands in his pockets. He looked confused. Maybe sad.

"You okay?" he asked.

"Yeah. Why?" Zena said.

"Because you weren't at the skating rink. I figured something was wrong." Adan tried to peek into the house, but Zena shifted her head to block him.

"Oh, that," Zena said vaguely. "I forgot."

"Forgot? But you seemed so excited."

"I was but, you know how it is. I just got busy."

"Oh." Adan's face went from maybe confused and maybe sad to definitely hurt.

Zena's heart sank. She hated her world for making her say what she'd said. She didn't want to hurt Adan. She was saying what she was saying because she wanted him to like her. Well, she didn't want him to not like her because her family was struggling and her mother wasn't a nurse and had to work overtime and she had to take care of her baby sister.

"Adan—"

"Zena—"

The two teenagers said each other's names at the same time as they tried to stumble out their feelings.

"You first," Adan said.

"No, you first," Zena countered.

"I'll just say this," Adan started with his voice cracking from its usual cool. "It's fine if you don't want to hang out and, like, be friends. I know school is starting soon and you'll make other friends. Okay? I know that. But I want to be your friend. I like you and I want to be your friend." He looked into Zena's eyes. "I really like you."

"Like, I like you, too," Zena blurted out clumsily.

The words were innocent enough, but the intentions had deep meaning behind them. What the two of them knew was their relationship had strengthened and left so much heightened emotional residue that they both laughed to lighten the moment.

"Hey, can I come in for a little while?" Adan asked.

"In here?"

"Yes. Into your house."

"Ohh." Zena looked over her shoulder as if maybe there was a circus breaking out in the living room behind her. She turned back to Adan. "You sure?" she asked him.

"Yes. I'm sure."

"Look, Adan. We don't have anything. I don't have a Nintendo like you do. Our television is on the floor," Zena said.

"That's fine," Adan answered in his cool tone. "I'm not here to play Nintendo or watch television. I'm here to see you."

"Ohh," Zena repeated. She stepped back and let Adan in. He kept her company and left right before her mother was to be home from work. That became their nightly ritual when her mother worked doubles. They swore Zola to secrecy and bribed her with Twix candy bars.

Zena was sure all of this would change when school started and all of the best friends Adan had, who frequently stopped by the house, got his attention before her. While she hadn't met any of the girls in the neighborhood, she imagined they'd all be prettier than her and have nicer bikes and already know all of the lyrics to the popular songs Adan played incessantly.

None of Zena's fears came to pass. Adan was also in the first-period history class where Zena sat beside Malak. One day when the teacher was absent and the substitute was late, the bored students started playing Twenty Questions, and Adan was selected first to sit in the hot seat in the center of the classroom. The girls led the questioning, asking if Adan was a virgin—he was and he admitted it—and soon Malak, who'd started the game for this very reason, asked if Adan had a girlfriend.

"Yes. I think so," Adan revealed, and the heartbreak from the girls in the room was palpable.

Malak pushed further: "Does she go to this school?" Adan nodded. "Is she in this classroom?" Adan nodded. "Is she wearing a red sweatshirt?" Adan nodded. All eyes moved to the only girl in that classroom who was wearing a red sweatshirt—the new girl. Zena.

When hungover and weary Zena could no longer ignore the sun rising outside her bedroom window, she decided to force herself out of bed. She suffered through her shower and pampering routine and stumbled through her condo trying not to remember Adan's face when he admitted that he liked her that night at her house.

When Zena finally made it out her front door and to her car, she decided she needed to make a stop before heading into the office, so she called

Malak to inform her of her extended late arrival. While Malak sounded surprised, Zena could also hear in her voice enthusiasm at the idea of her boss being out of the office a little while longer.

"Everything okay?" Malak asked with concern about the issues they'd confronted the night before laced in her tone.

"I'm fine," Zena said with forced brightness before adding rather dutifully, "Just email Judge Jones's assistant to let him know I won't make our appointment. I'll stop by the courthouse a little later, and I hope to catch him if he has time. And make sure those files from the new Patel case are entered into the system. I'll need them when I get in."

Zena could hear the sarcasm in Malak's voice when she replied, "I've already entered those files, and I'll send the email right away." Malak paused before adding, "Zena, I'm here if you want to talk about—"

"That will be all," Zena said, cutting Malak off as if she was a stranger trying to find her place in some tragedy she didn't understand. She hung up and exhaled through her mouth before jumping in her car to head to her mother's house.

Lisa Shaw still lived in the same little brick house in West End, Atlanta, she'd found refuge in after her divorce and escape from New York.

After years of haggling with the West Coast land-lord she'd never seen, Lisa purchased the modest property and was so proud of her achievement she went about the work of turning the little abode into an oasis in an enclave that was decent when she'd moved in with her family but declined through years of home owner flight, Section 8 hustles, weak property flips and foreclosures during the recession. But, Lisa, just happy to have her own land, held firm and refused to leave, even when Zena offered to purchase her mother a more lofty condo in town.

When Zena pulled into the driveway outside her mother's ranch house, she scanned the well-kept front garden packed with blooming perennials like the bog lily, the yellow flag iris and cannas. In the middle of the yard was a freshly painted white swinging garden bench Lisa forbade Zena and Zola or anyone else from ever sitting on. "That thing is just for show," Lisa said ten years ago when she had two day laborers she'd picked up in front of the Home Depot come and install it. "Got me a garden and a swing," Lisa said, stand-ing beside Zena and Zola that afternoon when the work was done. "Can you imagine that? A girl from 40 Projects? Got her own garden and swing!" She laughed and repeated her instructions: no one could ever sit on that swing.

Zena was about to use her old key to unlock

the front door, but it was already swinging open. Standing there was Lisa with her right hand on the knob and a lit cigarette in her left hand.

"Babygirl, your ears must be itching," Lisa said. She craned her neck over the threshold and looked past Zena toward the street, scanning the right and left side of the sidewalk. As usual, she was wearing one of the dozen dashikis Zena and Zola had gotten her for Kwanzaa. Her long gray dreadlocks were up in a bun, and her glasses were set low on her nose. While she was fifty-three and had endured what most would call a hard life, Lisa's appearance belied that fact. Beneath the gray dreadlocks, thick spectacles and frumpy house dress, she hadn't aged a day since they'd gotten off the bus in Atlanta.

"Itching? Why do you say that?" Instinctively, Zena turned and looked out at the street with her mother.

"I had a little visitor a few minutes ago," Lisa answered mysteriously as she backed up from the door to let Zena into the house.

"Zola? So she told you?" Zena charged, ready to argue her points against everything she'd come to her mother's house to discuss. Beginning her plea, she led her mother into the kitchen beside the front door, where most discussions occurred.

"No. Not Zola." Lisa laughed in a way that left a clue for Zena.

"Who?"

"You know." Lisa took a seat at the kitchen table beside Zena and put out her cigarette. While she'd stood firm in most of her fights with Zena about her smoking, reminding her firstborn that she was grown and Zena could not control smoking or anything else about her, she seemed like she was in no mood to have that fight again.

"Who was it, Mommy?" Zena pushed, though it was clear she'd read right into the clue.

"You know," Lisa repeated more firmly and enticingly.

Zena rushed to the bay window above the kitchen table and peered through the half-open blinds, careful not to reveal her position. "What? Why was he here? When was he here?" she asked, struggling to look up the street as if she could actually see anything five houses down where Roy Douglass, Adan and Alton's father, now lived alone after Mrs. Pam had died of breast cancer New Years Day.

"The usual," Lisa said. "Pretending he was here to check on me, but really trying to get news about you. You know these Southern men—so charming and a little manipulative." Lisa laughed. "He looked good. I don't see how you missed him. I swear he left just a few minutes before I saw you pull into the driveway."

Some tall teenage boy came into view, walking in the street in front of the house, and Zena thought for a second maybe it was Adan, so she jumped back, afraid her cover was blown, but then the baggy pants and basketball jersey proved otherwise.

"Asked about me? You didn't tell him anything. Right?" Zena looked back at Lisa.

"Don't start worrying. Lord! I told him the usual—I don't know anything. You don't tell me anything. Wasn't hard to say since it's the truth." Lisa's gaze cut to Zena.

"Mommy, don't go there." Zena plopped back into her seat like a teenager. She felt exhausted by everything—her mother's comment, Zola and the wedding, the idea of Adan lurking outside. What did he want anyway? Why was he always visiting her mother? She looked back at the window. She didn't feel like herself. She knew she didn't look like herself. She remembered being in the courtroom just twenty-four hours earlier. She was winning. She was what she wanted to be. Who she wanted to be. But now she was back at home in that little house and arguing with her mother.

"Don't go where? Ain't nowhere for me to go. I'm just an aging old lady, sitting at home and minding my business. You and your little teenage love are the ones who came knocking on my door," Lisa retorted.

"Fine. I didn't come here to talk about that man

anyway," Zena said snidely. "I don't care what he wants or why he was here."

"You sure don't sound like it. I thought you'd be over Adan by now, but I guess I also know that's impossible." Lisa grinned.

"First, we broke up in freaking college and I'm completely over him. Second, you know I've asked you not to say his name."

"Adan!" Lisa slapped her own lips playfully to punish herself for the intentional slip.

Zena ignored her comical routine and went on with her list: "And third, I don't care! I don't care! I don't care! And finally, like I said, that's not why I came here to talk to you."

"Well then why did you come to bless me with your presence, Ms. Zena Nefertiti Shaw?" Lisa joked.

"It's Zola. Did she tell you what she's planning to do?"

"What—you mean the wedding?"

"Yes. About eloping. So, she did tell you? You told her she couldn't do it, right?"

"No. Why would I do that?" Lisa asked.

"Because, it's crazy." Zena stared at her mother. Behind Lisa on the wall was a framed print of one of her many Gordon Parks pictures that were in the center of most walls throughout the house. This one was of a black girl standing before a whites-only water fountain. All through Zena's childhood, the picture inspired her to become a lawyer and fight injustices. "And because she's supposed to be studying for the Bar, so she can be an attorney," Zena went on. "And because you're her mother and you should be at her wedding."

"Oh, I don't care about that. She can do whatever she wants to do. She's twenty-five. I keep telling ya'll that. I've lived my life. You can't live for me. Got to live for yourself," Lisa said with too much Zen.

"That's ridiculous. Who doesn't want to see their daughter get married?"

"Who said anything about not wanting to see it? All I'm saying is that Zola is young and she's a free spirit. You know that," Lisa said. "I want her to have whatever she wants. Besides, I get it. I'm single and I don't have the best track record with marriage. Your father is up in New York doing God knows what, and then with Pam just passing from breast cancer four months ago, I see why Alton isn't trying to put his father through a wedding right now. Maybe it's best they elope. They're happy. Let them have some fun. We can always throw them a reception later."

"But what about her life? Her career? She could be making a huge mistake. You know the Bar Exam is in like eight weeks! She's talking about waiting to take it next year."

"She should be talking about not taking it at all," Lisa said.

"Why would you say that? After all she's done?"

"That's your dream, Zena. Not Zola's." Lisa stood to pour herself the last remaining cup of coffee from her electronic carafe.

"It's her dream, too. She finished law school and now she's set for the Bar. She's going to be an attorney." Zena looked at her mother sipping her coffee and grinning at her. "What? If she's not a lawyer, what will she be? What could she be?"

"Who the hell knows. Maybe Alton's wife?" Lisa laughed.

"I can't deal with you right now!" Zena stood and reached for her purse.

"Oh, you're going to run off now that I don't agree with everything you're saying?" Lisa said.

"I'm not running. I'm just frustrated. It's like in the last twenty-four hours all of this crazy stuff is happening. And I came here hoping you'd talk some sense into Zola, but it's like, as usual, you're on her side."

"I'm on no one's side. I just want peace. And I'm hoping to make you see Zola's side."

"Zola's side?" Zena laughed sarcastically. "Let me see—Zola's side includes eloping to Bali when the Exam is right around the corner. Zola's side includes getting married just when she's about to begin her career. I know all about Zola's side,

Mommy. I thought you'd see my side just this once."

Four eyes rolled, and Zena whisked out of the house in a way that was too common for her mother to be moved. Before Zena was in her car, Lisa had lit a new cigarette and was searching the kitchen table for the television remote. *Maury Povich* would be on in twenty minutes.

Zena made an aggressive right turn out of her mother's driveway—a turn away from Adan's old house. Her thoughts concocted a scenario where Adan was standing in his parents' front yard waiting for her to drive by. What did he want to say? Why had he asked about her? She gripped the head of the steering wheel and looked out the rearview window. The car slowed as she searched, deciding where he wasn't, which cars weren't his, which shadows in the bushes couldn't be his. Her emotions bullied her into forcing all thoughts of him away, so she resolved to snap herself back to "normal," but before she could refocus a glance to the driver's side door, her thoughts took her back—way back—to a memory that had taken place in that very location she was passing—the corner of Sassafras Street and Blue Stone Road.

It was junior year of high school. Zena and Adan were walking home from school. The dented Nissan Maxima Adan's parents got him when he turned sixteen was in the shop again, and while his best friend, Hakeem, volunteered to drive them home, Zena wanted to walk. She never minded walking home, not with Adan anyway. They could talk, really talk, about things in the world, things nobody else ever talked about, not at their school anyway. The longer she'd been around Adan she was learning that this was something that separated him from anyone she knew—he could talk about anything and seemed to know everything. And not in an annoying way, either. He was humble and charming. One afternoon, the two were walking hand in hand debating the possibility of love at first sight, a new concept Zena had encountered in a romance novel she found in the library at school. Zena said no, true love wasn't possible, and was completely dominating the conversation for a long while as Adan listened quietly, nodding from time to time. "It's ridiculous. Impossible. You can't love someone after seeing them just one time. Like one time?" Zena posed. "Like looking at someone doesn't let you know who they really are. They could be a horrible person. A liar. A killer. Right?"

Adan nodded again in acknowledgment of Zena's comment. "You just don't know someone. Like sometimes, I don't think you ever really know anyone. But definitely not from first sight. You don't know them enough to love them," Zena went on.

"But…" Adan began slowly before pausing to

gather his ideas. "But, what if it is possible? Like if it does happen for some people?"

Zena looked at Adan as if he'd gone crazy. "What kinds of people?"

Adan shrugged. "I don't know. Just, some people. Like, maybe us."

Zena laughed at the idea. "Us? You and me? Love at first sight?" She laughed again, though something in her stomach flipped the way it had when they'd met when her bicycle chain popped.

"Yes, us."

Adan let go of Zena's hand and took a few steps ahead of her so he could turn and face her. "You don't think we were love at first sight? You're saying you didn't feel anything when you first saw me? Nothing?"

Zena stopped walking and bit the inside of her upper lip to stop herself from smiling. She had felt something when she first laid eyes on Adan. But "love"? Was it love? Zena looked up at the street signs: Sassafras Street and Blue Stone Road. She readjusted her purse on her shoulder—Adan was carrying both of their book bags. Looking up at the signs, she said, "I did feel something."

Adan reached out and caught ahold of one of her hands. "Me, too. I felt something, too," he admitted.

The hold Zena had on her upper lip failed, and

a huge smile was produced on her face, one that was so big, it almost hurt her cheeks.

"What? What's so funny?" Adan asked. Standing there in his Aeropostale sweatshirt and with his and Zena's fake matching Benetton knapsacks hanging from his back, Adan looked so nervous, as if he was starting a conversation he'd never wanted to have.

"Nothing. I'm not laughing. I'm just smiling. Smiling and wondering," Zena said.

"Wondering what?"

"I'm wondering if you're saying you love me. If we're in love," Zena said.

Just then everything went black. The sky first and then everything around Zena and Adan went to shadows as if night had come from nowhere. Adan grabbed Zena's hand—not as if he was scared, but just automatically, as if it had been his first instinct to hold on to her, to protect her. "What's happening?" she asked, spinning around. It was just three-fifteen in the afternoon but no one was outside in their neighborhood. Not one dog was barking. No cars were speeding by in the road blasting music. It was dark and quiet.

"I don't know," Adan answered, turning, too. At some point, while he was holding Zena's hand, the two were back-to-back surveying their surroundings. It was the year 2000, and cell phones hadn't become a thing yet. The only way they could get anyone's attention was to scream. But something told them not to. Something told them everything was fine. Adan looked up at the sky. That's when he saw it. The moon—right in broad daylight. "Look," was all he said.

And feeling his head tilted back behind her, Zena looked up, too. After staring for a while, Zena uttered, "It's beautiful. It's an eclipse."

Chins up, ear to ear, hands still clasped from behind, Zena and Adan stared at the moon as if it was their first time seeing it, as if it was a pearl pinned to the sun. Everything beneath the sky disappeared. They were floating astronauts, space twins, drifting in a celestial storm of miracles somewhere between Earth and the heavens.

At school the next day, Zena and Adan told their science teacher, Mr. Palabas, what happened to them the prior afternoon. He was one of those spunky, white, hip earth science teachers who spent far too much time at the school trying to get the students he taught to understand that science was interesting and applicable and cool. When they talked to Mr. Palabas, he acknowledged there hadn't been an eclipse—including the fact that he had not seen one. The rookie science teacher nodded along as Adan and Zena recalled their story before beginning to let them down gently. From the bookshelf behind his messy desk, he pulled a textbook that weighed more than a toddler and flipped through pages with recorded eclipse dates in the past and future predictions. There were no predictions for April 14, 2000. Without saying it, Mr. Palabas was implying a scientific reality: there had been no eclipse.

"So you don't believe us?" Zena asked as more kids started filing into the room for class to begin.

"I believe you two experienced an eclipse," Mr. Palabas answered.

"But was there an eclipse—an actual eclipse of the sun?" Adan asked.

"Not according to these books—not according to science. But that doesn't mean you didn't experience one. Maybe it was your eclipse. An eclipse just for you two," Mr. Palabas said, and Zena and Adan looked at each other.

After switching from her driving flats to her red-bottom pumps, Zena walked into the lobby of the Peachtree skyscraper, where she rented a small but extravagant space with floor-to-ceiling windows and complementary plush leather office furniture. She promised herself she wouldn't bring up the wedding or Zola or her mother and definitely not Adan as she got off the elevator on the tenth floor. But when she saw Malak sitting at her desk in the reception area, everything she'd been hoping to hold inside came up and out her mouth the way secrets and gossip force their way to the surface when best friends resume company.

Zena leaned into Malak's desk and just started.

"Can you believe he went to my mother's house looking for me again?" She paused but went on with no answer from Malak, who was in the middle of a conversation with the phone receiver to her ear. "I mean, what the hell? What do you want from me? Why are you looking for me? Just because our sister and brother are getting married doesn't mean we are suddenly besties and you can just roll up at my mother's house," Zena said as if she was suddenly talking to Adan, but then she switched back to Malak with, "Can you believe that? Can you believe that mess? Wait, girl. Are you on the phone? Never mind. Sorry."

Malak slid the phone onto her desk and looked up at Zena with little surprise. "I'm off now," Malak said. "And, yeah, I know he was looking for you."

Zena dropped her workbag to the floor. "How?"

"He came here," Malak revealed.

Zena looked around as if maybe he was still in her office hiding out. "Here?"

"Yes."

Zena reached over the desk and grabbed the sides of Malak's arms like she was a reluctant witness to some atrocity. "What? Are you kidding me? He was here? What did he want? Why was he here?" She shook her friend.

"Clearly, he was looking for you."

Malak raised her arms to break from Zena's hold. She was used to Zena losing all composure when these kinds of things happened. In fact, she'd already told herself that she wouldn't bring Adan's pop-in visit up, but since Zena had already opened that door, all promises of silence had been recanted. "Calm down, Z," she said. "He was just downtown and wanted to talk to you. I think it's about the wedding or something." Malak grinned. "He looked good, too. Smelled good. Had on one of those fancy suits. He obviously wanted to impress someone— and it wasn't me." She sucked her teeth playfully.

"I don't care how he looked. He isn't my man," Zena said defiantly as she slid into the seat before Malak's desk—a clear sign she wanted more information. "But what did he say? I need to know everything he said."

Malak went through Adan's visit second by second for her best friend—how he'd said, "Ze-ena"; how he looked crestfallen when Malak revealed that Zena hadn't showed up at the office just yet; that he said he was in town looking for a new office space; that he was bringing his practice to Georgia. He was tired of the New York hustle and wanted to be closer to his dad. Malak shared her condolences about his mother passing and he'd looked down at the floor. He changed the subject quickly, told her she didn't have to tell Zena he'd stopped by. He'd see Zena soon. He'd make sure he did this time.

Zena froze with her mouth open and heart beating wildly. "What?" she managed to get out. "He said that? Are you sure he said that—like exactly?"

"No, I'm crazy, I made it up. I made it all up," Malak teased but then added, "Of course, I didn't fabricate this story. Why would I do that? He said it. All of it."

"Why? Why would he say that? Why does he want to see me?" Zena asked.

"I have no answers—only information. Good information, though. But, like I said, it seemed like he wanted to talk about the wedding."

"The wedding? Why do we need to talk about that?"

"Again, I have no answers, but I'm guessing it's about you being the maid of honor and him being the best man," Malak said. "Maybe he wants to go half on a gift with you. Or maybe he doesn't want them to get married, either. Maybe he's just as pissed off about all of this as you are and needs to vent."

Zena pondered. "But, still, why talk to me about it? Not like I can stop it." She scowled as she recalled the last conversation with her sister. "I don't even want to think about this. And I sure don't want to talk about it with Adan. Shouldn't he go vent to someone else if he has an issue? Someone like his wife?"

While she'd been nodding along with all of her friend's commentary, the last question gave Malak pause. She looked at Zena like she'd misspoke. "His wife?" Malak repeated as if Zena knew something she didn't or maybe Zena was confused or just wrong. "What do you mean 'his wife'?"

"His wife!" Zena shot back solidly like there was no way Malak couldn't know exactly what she'd been talking about. "His wife! Adan's wife! That's who he should be talking to. Right?"

"Talking to his wife who?" Malak's furrowed brow confirmed further confusion.

"His wife! The woman he married. That doctor— the surgeon in New York," Zena said so confidently, she sounded like she was identifying the color of the sky.

"What wom—" Malak stopped herself and directly said to Zena, "He never married that chick. Adan's not married—not unless you know something I don't know."

"He married her. It was in the damn *New York Times*!"

"No—their engagement was in the *New York Times*. But not the wedding. They never got married."

Zena felt all the blood in her body leave her

extremities and flood her brain. Her heart quivered. Something behind her eyes turned red, and she felt like she could faint—if she didn't have to hold on to ask Malak more questions. She had to be certain she was hearing what she was hearing. What was she hearing? Adan not married? Not married? Not married three years ago and probably on his second child by now? Moved on from her and into his life, a suburban dad with a suburban wife and life that was comprised of elegant dinner parties in the Hamptons and Paris vacations? What? What the hell?

"But he was engaged and it was in the newspaper! He was supposed to marry her! Why didn't he? Why didn't you tell me?" Zena looked somewhere between bewildered and amazed.

"Tell you? I'm not even supposed to mention his name. Remember that? You forbid me from ever saying his name after that *Times* article came out," Malak said.

"But my mother? Zola? No one has said anything to me about it. Why didn't you tell me? Why didn't anyone tell me?"

"Z, you forbid all of us from saying anything about Adan."

"Who cares about me forbidding you? You never listen to me any other time. And I'd think you'd know this was big enough to tell me. You can't just have me walking around in the world thinking my ex-boyfriend is married and he isn't!"

"But you said you didn't care. Remember? You said you couldn't care less about anything he was doing. He was so far in your past you hardly remembered anything about him," Malak recalled, sharing the fake sentiments as dully as Zena had. "Plus, I figured you knew anyway. That you would get the information the way everyone else gets information about their ex." Malak picked up her phone, unlocked it and handed it to Zena with a blue screen flashing. "Facebook," she said, leading Zena to Adan's page.

"Single!" Zena read aloud on his profile. She clicked into his pictures and scrolled through. There he was, all brown and peering into her. He'd aged, grown into something more distinctive, distinguished like his father and his uncles. Had a short fade and expensive-looking spectacles. He looked like the kind of man who read the newspaper at a coffee shop every morning, as if maybe he was a professor or a UN ambassador. He was handsome. The perfect depiction of what he wanted to be. In one picture he was sitting on a couch reading a book. In another, he was standing a few feet left of the Leaning Tower of Pisa. Zena quickly wondered who'd taken the pictures.

"So, you're saying you've never looked at this

page?" Malak inquired, surprised by what she knew was the answer. "It's public. It's like…public."

"No. Why would I?" Zena asked.

"Because he's your ex. I look at all of my exes' pages on Facebook. I even look at my exes' exes' pages."

"I don't have time for that. I'm too busy with this." Zena looked around the office suggestively. "I can't worry myself with what's happening to Adan. I wasn't trying to get my feelings—" Zena stopped herself.

Malak completed her thought. "Hurt?" she offered.

"No—confused," Zena corrected her. "I didn't want to get *confused* by whatever *this* is." She flippantly flicked the phone back onto Malak's desk and jumped up to regain her composure.

"It's the truth—reality—you know, what you've been avoiding all these years," Malak said.

"Don't start!" Zena picked up her bag and started walking toward her office. "I'm not avoiding reality. I'm avoiding Adan. Totally different."

"Sure you're right," Malak said, unconvinced.

"Of course I'm right," Zena said. "Look, I'm done with this. I'm letting it roll off my back." She smiled obnoxiously and pretended to shake invisible feathers on her back. "I'm feeling great. I'm ready to get on with my day and move on from all of this nonsense. I'm going to my office to look over these Patel files, and then I'm heading over to the courthouse to try to catch Judge Jones. Can you email his assistant so they're expecting me?"

"About that meeting—"

"What?"

"Zola called. She's going to get fitted for a dress today, and she wanted you to go along with her. I think she wants you to pick out a dress, too, or something," Malak revealed.

"Today?" Zena looked down at her watch. "I can't do that today. What, she thinks because she decided to get married in like forty-eight hours I need to rush and change my whole schedule to be at her beck and call? No way. I am an important attorney, and I have things to do—none of which include picking out a wedding dress."

"Actually you don't have anything to do," Malak said nervously.

"Nothing? What do you mean, nothing?"

"I cleared your schedule."

"The hell? Why would you do that?"

"Because this is more important," Malak said, standing up to meet her best friend eye to eye. "Because you said you would at least try to support your sister. And because she needs you. And because I love her. And because I love you."

The sweet statements at the end softened the impact of Malak's actions.

"Please give me the strength to be a fence!"

Zena shouted in disgust before turning to her office. "I need a barrier to stop me from screaming at somebody this morning."

Chapter 3

Zola was standing on the sidewalk in front of the big shop window at Madame Lucille's Lace, one of the last black-owned couture bridal boutiques in Atlanta. On display in the window was an elegant, slender brown mannequin draped in crystal-lined lace and organza that swept the floor. A Mississippi transplant with a French name and fake French accent, Madame Lucille Archambeau was known for making dramatic, big-entry wedding gowns that piqued the interest of the city's new elite ladies who used their wedding day to make a statement about who they were and where they were going.

When Zena pulled into the parking lot at Lucille's, still rolling her eyes at the idea of participating in the dress selection and fitting, she noted how small and humble her baby sister looked standing before the bedecked mannequin. She was so lanky, so svelte, her frame seemed smaller than the mannequins. Zola was sporting her common puffy topknot, vintage pink bifocals, weathered white high-top Chuck Taylors and secondhand-store clothing. She was boho chic, pipsqueak cute, no frills and no Atlanta fly girl fashion. Just beautiful without trying to be. But fragile and small. Too delicate. So delicate, Zena almost felt bad for her standing there by herself. If she didn't know Zola, she'd wonder where her people were—where her friends were. If anyone cared a thing about her.

"You came!" Zola called to Zena when she spotted her walking toward the building from the parking lot. Zola had been thumbing through her phone; she looked as if she might have been calling Zena. She quickly stashed the phone into the hobo sack on her arm and embraced Zena. "I can't believe you came. Malak said she'd make you, but I can't believe she really did!"

Zena let Zola wrap her arms around her, but Zena kept her arms straight and at her sides. She could smell weed and some spicy perfume in Zola's hair. It reminded her of when Zola started smoking marijuana in high school. Zena had discovered her stash beneath the sink in the bathroom they shared between their bedrooms. Zena was home for spring break and needed to borrow one of Zola's tampons, but when she pulled out the box, a rather large Ziploc bag of marijuana fell to the floor.

"Malak can't make me do a damn thing," Zena said as Zola let her go at Lucille's.

"So you came on your own accord?" Zola grinned.

"I came, Zol. I just came. Okay?" Zena said flatly. "I'm saying, what more could you want from me? Just last night you told me about the wedding, and today you're picking out wedding dresses. It's a bit much—and a bit fast."

"Well, I have two weeks, and Madame Lucille was the only couture dressmaker who said she could have something ready."

"A rush order? Sounds expensive." Zena pointed out. "How are you paying for this?"

"No worries. It's a gift," Zola said grinning. "And you don't even have to worry about your dress, either. All covered."

"Well, I know it's not Mommy. And where is she? Isn't that how this is supposed to go? Like, your mother should be here, right?" Zena asked. There was no reason to add friends to that list. Zola never really had many friends. Growing up, Zola always complained that the girls in their neighborhood were too shallow or too mean. She preferred her books of poetry and her Alton.

Zola stepped back and looked up the street pensively. "I invited Mommy. But she claimed she had things to do in her garden and that I could do it myself. You know how she is. Ever since Daddy—" Zola stopped herself and looked back at Zena as if there was something she was about to say that both of them knew but neither really wanted to hear. She went on, leaving gaps where those words might be. "If she doesn't want to be here, I'm fine with that. I don't want to deal with her pessimism anyway. That's part of why Adan and I decided to elope. I can't deal with all of her negativity. *She* can't deal with all of her baggage."

While Zena's scowl hadn't dissipated, these words served as a bridge to her sister's emotional landscape and softened Zena's antagonism. She knew her mother's limitations too well, and although Zena always managed to live with them, to put them aside and continue to press forward, Zola saw her mother's shortcomings as short circuits in their own relationship. While Zena took Lisa's ever-swelling pain at her husband's betrayal as revelation of what came with loving someone, Zola internalized Lisa's disdain for their father as slight disdain for them, for her in particular.

Soon, Madame Lucille, a silver fox decked out in a black cashmere duster and thick black Dior lenses, came out of the dress shop chiding the sisters for loitering in front of her business and, worse, blocking the couture vision in the display window. When the sisters revealed that Zola was the bride, Madame Lucille snapped her fingers, and two perky assistants dressed in all black appeared from nowhere to whisk Zola into the empty shop, where they busied her with a bin of fabric swatches and photo albums.

One of the assistants took Zena's measurements. Madame Lucille reappeared with a sketch pad and began talking about Zena's bone structure, the length of her arms, the width of her ankles as she sketched what looked like a bunch of scribbling from Zena's perspective. After what felt like seconds, Madame Lucille exhaled as if she'd run a mile and dropped her pencil to the floor. Without conferring with Zena, who was leaning forward from the hold of the assistant with the measuring tape to get a peek at the dress sketch, Madame Lucille shared her work with Zola.

"I love it! I love it so much!" Zola squealed before looking at Zena. "Oh, my God! You're going to look fabulous."

Zena smiled and tried again to get a look at the sketch herself, but one step away from the assistant measuring her led to the woman mistakenly jabbing a straight pin into Zena's thigh.

"Ouch!" Zena hollered as Madame Lucille left the room with the sketch.

After Zola picked out a few bridal gowns from the look book, one of the assistants brought a stuffed rolling wardrobe into the showroom, and Zena sat on a plush cream parlor settee as Zola was tugged in and out of dresses that looked half-right and all wrong. Madame Lucille peeked over her glasses and gave adamant "no's," scolding her assistants as if they were the reason for the trouble finding something perfect for Zola.

Zena watched Zola's confusion in the scene and thought of what she had been doing this time of year when she was Zola's age. Along with some of her classmates from Howard, she'd locked herself up in a hotel room out by the airport and studied so long and so hard for the Bar Exam that when she closed her eyes, she could see the pages from her study guides burned into her pupils. While the room smelled stale and the delivery pizza got really old really fast, the dedication to passing the exam was addictive to Zena. The focus required that she leave thoughts of everything else, of everyone behind. She didn't have to worry. All she needed to do was focus. And soon that focus would pay off and fix everything that once worried her.

The only thing that kept threatening to splinter Zena's focus in that hotel room six years ago was the knowledge that somewhere in New York,

Adan was probably doing the same thing. Law school had been their dream together. On one of those long walks home from school, they decided they'd open a practice together. The name was to be something like Law: From A to Z, which Zena hated, but Adan's enthusiasm made it minimally appealing. They'd take on civil rights cases like Thurgood Marshall and Johnny Cochrane. The plan was to graduate from high school, go to Spelman and Morehouse, then they were off to Harvard Law. They would work part-time so they didn't rack up student-loan debt, return to Georgia to take the Bar and then Law: From A to Z would be born.

Adan made it all sound so simple in the love letters he passed to Zena in the hallway at school. But then Zena didn't get into Spelman, and Adan got a full scholarship to Morehouse. Resourceful, he changed the plan. He'd take the full Morehouse scholarship. Zena would go to Bethune-Cookman. They'd see each other on breaks and in four years meet up at Harvard. But then that didn't go as planned.

Adan got into Harvard, but Zena wasn't accepted, and while she'd gotten into some top-tier law schools, she loved her Historically Black College experience at Bethune-Cookman and how Howard's law alumni in Georgia began courting her when she'd been accepted. So after seven years together, lots of leaning on and dreaming, two weeks before college graduation, Adan showed up at Zena's off-campus apartment talking all philosophically about their relationship and love and what people have had to do to survive through the centuries.

Zena ignored most of this. She was used to Adan's speeches. His big ideas and pontificating. She sat at her kitchen table, eyeing her thick Howard acceptance folder and half listened as a girlfriend would. As Adan paced and talked about excellence and "keeping his eyes on the prize," she watched him and remembered the first day they met. How cute he was. That he stole her air. The butterflies. That night after the football game junior year in Jason Corbin's basement when she lost her virginity to Adan.

She remembered their long talks, talks just like this, where they figured things out, understood things, revealed their deepest secrets in whispers. Adan had been the only person she could talk to about her parents' divorce, how it felt to suddenly not have a father there every morning—how it felt to have him ripped from her life. What it was like to watch her mother waste entire weekends in bed, smoking and watching *Dallas* reruns. And even when Lisa managed to get up and out and meet someone, it would be weeks before she'd discover he was in a relationship or just emotionally unavailable. Soon, Zena watched as Lisa gave up and resolved to stay in bed, or as close to bed as possible.

Adan was the only person who would listen to this and drape his arm over her shoulders before kissing her cheek. That was when he was a boy, but standing there in her kitchen, Adan was a full-grown man. Maybe this meant all men weren't all bad and unreliable. And love was something she could trust. Not all marriages were like the ones she'd seen in New York, like her parents'. Some were good. Mrs. Pam and Mr. Roy were in love, always in love. For the first time, Zena wondered if she'd always be in love with Adan. If he'd be her husband and they'd be married.

But then she heard Adan say something.

"So we should just be friends," Zena remembered hearing Adan say that afternoon in her apartment, miles from Bethune-Cookman.

She watched the assistants stuff Zola into another horrible dress and remembered Adan standing there, his arms crossed, his eyes focused and serious. But he couldn't be serious. He couldn't. But he went on. "I'm going to be in Boston and you will be in DC. It won't be like Atlanta and Florida. You won't be home on weekends and I won't be able to stop everything to spend time with you. Look, we have to focus right now. We have to get this right, Z. We can't afford to lose."

Zena remembered feeling her chest grow warm

and looking at Adan as if he was slipping away and suddenly a million miles in the distance. "Lose what? Lose us?" Zena had asked, confused.

"No," Adan answered. "I mean lose sight of your dreams. Of where we are going and how that could benefit our people. We have to put that first, Z. We have to put that before ourselves. And who knows, maybe when we make it, we can get back together, but until then, I think it's over. I think we have to let this thing go."

Zola was standing in front of Zena, complaining about something. None of the dresses were working, and she was running out of options.

"What do you think I should do?" Zola asked in the middle of her lament, but Zena didn't know how to respond, as she hadn't been listening.

Zena took a sip from the bottle of Perrier one of the assistants had placed on the glass table beside the settee.

"She's getting annoyed," Zola said, pointing to Madame Lucille, who was pulling dresses from the racks and tossing them to the floor while admonishing her assistants in French for bringing them to the showroom. "I can't afford to mess this up. I don't have time to go somewhere else. But nothing is sticking. Nothing looks like me—you know? The dresses are too big and fluffy or too slender and elegant. I don't think I'm any of those things. I guess I don't know what I am."

Zola fell onto the settee beside Zena and leaned forward, resting her elbows on her knees.

"Maybe I'm in over my head. Maybe that's what this dress thing is about. Like, I'm rushing so nothing is working," she said helplessly.

Zena sighed audibly at her sister's inconsistencies. While the sudden sadness was new for free-spirited Zola, the flip-flopping wasn't. For the first time, Zena got the inkling that maybe the wedding didn't have to go down; that maybe there was something she could do to stop it. She could use Zola's indecisiveness to get her to see things the way Zena saw them; or at least get Zola to hold out long enough to pass the Exam and then have more options.

"You might be right." Zena fed the idea to Zola softly beneath Madame Lucille's fake French chattering with the assistants about what to put on the wardrobe next.

"You think so?" Zola asked, her eyes widening on Zena.

"I promised myself I wouldn't say anything else, since you've obviously made up your mind, but maybe this is a sign."

Heat from outside rushed toward the sisters, signaling that the shop door had opened. They turned to see a familiar figure walking toward them, but the harsh rays of the sun coming in from the display window splashed in over most of the features.

"Who is it? You can't come in here now! We have a private appointment!" Madame Lucille protested, walking toward the figure with her assistants behind her.

"I was invited," the person said, and Zola jumped to her feet.

"Mommy!" she yelped and ran to her mother for relief. "You came."

"Yes. Last minute, but I came," Lisa said, walking past Madame Lucille. She was wearing a sweat suit, a hot pink Wal-Mart jogger that she refused to give up though it was shrinking and losing shape. "I thought you girls needed me right now. Lord knows what would happen if I left you alone doing this."

Zola pulled Lisa to the settee as if she was joining a slumber party. Along the way, Madame Lucille greeted her as the mother of the bride and snapped for the assistants to bring her something to drink.

Zola pointed to all of the dresses she'd picked over, the ones she was sure she'd love and the ones she hated but tried anyway. She went into the speech she'd just given Zena about maybe making the wrong decision, but Lisa was obviously unmoved by her child's confusion. In the middle of Zena and Zola, Lisa looked around the shop and saw a mannequin toward the back in a thin rose-gold lace sheath that looked more like a cocktail dress than something a bride would say vows in.

"Try that one," Lisa said, pointing to the dress knowingly.

All eyes shifted to the back of the shop and then back to Lisa as if she was crazy.

"No, Madame! It's not enough," Madame Lucille argued, wagging her index finger at the simple design. "It doesn't have enough *gravitas*. It's not for the bride."

"Well, maybe not for all brides, but I think it may fit this one." Lisa slid her hand onto Zola's knee.

"Really? You really think so?" Zola kind of tilted her head toward the dress. It really was nice. Simple, but nice. Pretty and dainty. She stood and walked to the mannequin with her hands held out, set to grab hold of her mother's suggestion.

Minutes later, all in the shop would see that mother really does know best. Lisa's simple suggestion looked easy on Zola. When she stepped out of the dressing room in the rose-gold sheath, which looked whimsical, soft and romantic against Zola's mahogany skin, Madame Lucille covered her mouth as if she was about the cry.

"Magnifique! Magnifique!" Madame Lucille shouted. "It's perfect. Like it was made for you, *mademoiselle*! We can add some layering, a little fall from the shoulders. But I love it!"

"I know! I know!" Zola was back to her giddy self, nearly dancing her way to the fitting pedestal. "I love it, too!"

Zena watched her sister's glee as she floated by in rose gold. Zena always thought the talk about the moment the bride finding "her" dress and bringing everyone in the room to tears was a bunch of crap. It was just a dress. But in that moment, looking at Zola, she felt some of that sappiness. Lisa's selection made all the other dresses look silly. It was somehow an expression, an extension of Zola's beauty that pushed her into some new status of womanhood. It made Zena's thoughts toss through memories of Zola growing into her femininity: her first time wearing Zena's lip gloss, her first lace bra, Zena twisting Zola's hair up in a bun before her first high school dance.

As Zola posed for Lisa, Zena felt something like tears creeping up the backs of her eyes, but she held them back.

"You love it, Zena?" Zola asked.

"It's okay," Zena offered. "Nice."

It was a weak approval but enough for Zola, who turned and went back to smile at herself in the mirror behind the pedestal. The assistants went on pinning the dress to her thin frame for proper alterations and some personalized touches from the swatches Zola liked, and Madame Lucille assured

Zola she'd personally handle everything within the next three days.

After hearing this, when the fitting was done and everyone naturally gathered at the front of the shop, Zena inquired about the dress Madame Lucille quickly sketched on a pad for her.

"It's special," Zola said. "I wanted you to have something really special."

"But it's your wedding. Shouldn't you be in the special dress?" Zena asked.

"I know, but you've always been way more fabulous than me," Zola explained.

"Well, how much does it cost?" Zena asked Zola, remembering that Madame Lucille had promised to make and fix a dress in just days. "How much is all of this costing?"

"I already told you—don't worry about it," Zola said.

"It's taken care of," Madame Lucille said, and the tone of her voice made it clear that some astronomical fee she'd imposed had cleared someone's bank account.

"Taken care of? By whom?" Zena asked, looking to Lisa suspiciously, but she knew there was no way she could pay the thousands it was likely costing to cover these charges. "Who is paying?"

"Me."

A male voice shot into the small shop like a flock of seagulls suddenly taking flight. The door was wide-open as if it had always been that way, and in the frame stood a person, a being that brought a bounty of confusing sensations to Zena's body and mind. She was stimulated by the sight, excited, awakened, pulled to life the way anyone would feel seeing an old friend, but then she was angered and agitated, dragged through the past the way anyone would feel when that old friend was an ex-boyfriend.

"Adan!" Zola cheered, bulleting past Zena and jumping into Adan's arms, as if he was a big brother returned home from the war.

Lisa looked on, smiling, but Zena could feel her mother's eyes somehow focusing on her.

In fact, Zena felt as if everyone's eyes were on her at that moment—the assistants', Madame Lucille's, even God in heaven who'd stopped time so everyone in the shop could also hear her heart beating, her throat closing and her spinning thoughts: the shop suddenly smelled like the cologne Adan wore in college; his eyes were the same; his smile was so big. He looked happy. Why hadn't he gotten married? Why was he there? He was too handsome. How'd he get to be so handsome? He really wasn't married? There was no wedding band on his ring finger.

Zena pursed her lips tightly as if these thoughts were in danger of being spoken aloud. And though she'd relaxed a little and admitted that neither her mother nor Madame Lucille and her assistants were looking at her, there was no denying where Adan had set his eyes. They were on Zena.

"Z, I've been looking for you," he said really casually.

"Guess you found me," Zena replied, mocking his tone.

"The groom?" Madame Lucille asked, stepping between them and sort of grinning at Adan.

"No. I'm the best man." Adan shook Madame Lucille's hand. "I'm Adan Douglass. We actually spoke on the phone earlier."

Madame Lucille smiled. "Oh, yes. The financier. My favorite person in the room."

"That's me," Adan confirmed. "I just wanted to stop by to make sure everything was satisfactory with the payment."

"Everything is fine, Mr. Douglass," Madame Lucille said. "I just need your signature on a few things and we're all set."

Zena watched as Adan followed Madame Lucille to the register just a few feet away.

"He's paying for this?" Zena asked Zola.

"Yes. My wedding gift. Isn't that great?"

"No. It's not."

"Why?" Zola asked.

Zena watched Adan chatting and joking with Madame Lucille at the register as if he must be up to something sinister. "Because I don't want him paying for my dress. I can pay for my own dress. I can pay for your dress, too!"

Zola looked confused, but Lisa stood there glowering at Zena for her petty resistance.

"Really? But I thought you didn't want to pay for anything," Zola said.

"I never said that," Zena countered.

"Yes, you did," Zola argued.

"No, I didn't."

"Yes, you did!"

"No, I—"

"Girls!" Lisa jumped in just as Adan had made his way back to their circle, stuffing his credit card into his wallet.

The assistants had gone about their work in the shop, and Madame Lucille was on the telephone.

"All clear," Adan announced.

"That's wonderful," Lisa said. "And thank you so much for supporting Alton and Zola. I know how much they appreciate you."

"Of course. I've been watching those two fall in love since—" Adan paused. "I guess 1999 when you all moved to Atlanta."

"You remember the actual *year*?" Lisa asked, smiling with surprise.

"I'll never forget it," he replied before looking at Zena. "Changed everything."

Adan escorted the women out of the shop. Zena followed behind, watching everyone walk and listening to them talk with a frown on her face. She scanned Adan's body. He was wearing loose-fitting jeans and a fitted white T-shirt that showed off his chest. His arms were muscular and smooth.

"So, what's going on with the case you were telling me about—the one with the little boy from Brooklyn who was abused by his foster parents?" Zena heard her mother ask Adan. She squinted and rolled her eyes at Lisa.

"We got him some help," Adan answered.

"Help? I don't care about that. Did you win? Did you sue the state?" Lisa prodded.

Adan laughed and added, "We did, Mrs. Shaw. I didn't want to put it like that, but we did. He's on a long, tough road to recovery mentally, but financially, he's secure for the rest of his life."

"That's amazing. We need more good lawyers out there like you, doing what you do. Every time you call and tell me you've won a case, I cheer because I know you're on the right side of things," Lisa said.

Zena read into her mother's words and concluded that Lisa and Adan chatted regularly. This was news to Zena. It was also interesting that Lisa knew what Adan was doing in his career. The last she'd heard, he'd followed his dream of working in civil rights but also took on some smaller pro bono community cases. His firm was small but successful. He was in the headlines, but Zena struggled not to catch any of them. Apparently, Lisa wasn't doing the same. She sounded as if Adan was her long-lost son.

"Thank you for saying that. I need to hear it every once in a while," Adan said to Lisa. "Things get hectic working in the community. I mean, it pays well in the heart, but it stresses the head and wallet." Adan looked at Zena. "I'm sure you understand, Zena."

Before Zena could respond, Lisa answered for her, saying, "Please, Zena works with rich people. Her clients are trying to add millions to their millions."

"Not true, Mommy," Zena said. "I take on some pro bono work, too."

"Really?" Zola looked at Zena as if this was a stretch.

Zena snapped back, "Yes, really."

"See, I knew you'd work with the people," Adan said, catching Zena's eye and locking in. "That was your dream. It was our dream. Remember?"

Zena didn't say anything. She was silent until the lull in the conversation was deafening.

Lisa announced that she had to get going. She was working the night shift at the airport. Adan volunteered to walk Lisa to her car, but she wouldn't have it.

Zena tried to follow Lisa and Zola into the parking lot without saying goodbye to Adan, but he stopped her.

"Zena, hey, can I talk to you for a second?" he asked.

The question split the air. All three of the women stopped. Zola and Lisa looked at Zena, anticipating her response with nervous excitement.

"Me?" Zena looked as if maybe she'd heard him incorrectly or maybe there was another Zena within a hundred-mile radius.

"Yeah. *You*."

Zena looked at Adan discerningly, but she didn't respond.

After a few seconds of silence, Lisa said, "Of course you can, Adan," while reaching out for Zena. "But first, let me chat with her and Zola. I just need to make sure the girls are ready for our family dinner party."

"Dinner party?" Zola asked as Lisa pulled her and Zena to the side and forced them into a huddle.

"What dinner party, Mommy?" Zola repeated.

"Shut up, child. There ain't no damn dinner party," Lisa said bluntly. "I pulled you two here because I wanted to say something to you girls and I want to make sure I say it before I leave here. Now, I know I haven't been the best mother—the best role model. I never really got over your daddy cheating on me and that divorce. But I don't want you two to use that as a way to limit yourselves.

Love is a beautiful thing. And you can't be afraid of it. I haven't found anyone. But that doesn't mean you can't."

Lisa looked at Zola and said, "It doesn't mean you can't get married." Lisa looked at Zena and said, "And it doesn't mean you can't fall in love." She closed her eyes, and a tear rolled down each cheek. "I want you girls to support each other in love. To make sure you both find it. And keep it. And protect it. Even if I can't help you, I can tell you the truth." Lisa kissed Zola on the forehead, and then she went to kiss Zena, but before she did, she said sternly, "Don't mess this up. That man loves you."

"Mommy—" Zena started, but Lisa stopped her.

"No excuses! Just listen to me," Lisa ordered.

When Zola and Lisa left, Zena stood there facing the parking lot, watching them pull out in their cars, afraid to turn around to face Adan. She felt as if maybe he wasn't really there. Maybe this wasn't real. She'd imagined him walking into the shop. Imagined him walking out.

"I'm still here," Adan said as if he had been reading her mind. "Right over here." He waved jokingly.

At once, Zena felt Adan behind her. She could smell him. See his shadow above hers on the concrete. This only made it harder to turn around.

"You going to walk away or something?" Adan asked softly, and it might have been a joke but he sounded as if it was plausible.

Zena turned swiftly, ready for battle or confrontation. "No, Adan," she said. "I'm not going to walk away—not yet. So what did you want to talk about?"

"Are you free? Maybe we could go somewhere to get a drink."

"Why? What do you need to say to me over a drink that you can't say right here?" Zena asked harshly.

"Dang, girl," Adan said, responding to her gruffness. "I was just suggesting we go somewhere to get out of this heat. But I guess I do remember that you like being outside in the middle of the afternoon."

"Look, I don't have time for a drink. I need to get back to my office. I have work to do."

"I thought Malak said your day was clear," Adan said.

"Really? She told you that? I guess she's also the person who told you I'd be here."

"No. I didn't expect to see you here. I was just stopping by to make sure Zola was all right."

"Why? Why are you doing this? Why are you paying for her dress?" Zena asked.

"It's a gift. And why not?" Adan answered.

"Because." Zena slid her hand onto her hip and

furrowed her brow to bring the past into the discussion.

"Because we haven't spoken?" Adan asked.

"That's the understatement of the century."

"But this is about Alton and Zola. I want to support them. I thought we both should. That's why I want to talk to you—to find out where your head is on Bali and everything."

"Oh. That's what you wanted to talk to me about?" Zena asked. Just then, the heat had gotten to her. She felt sweat rolling down her back, her underarms moisten. The anxiety in her gut was bubbling up. She wanted to scream at Adan. Did he really think he was going to show up and just talk about Zola's wedding? Without talking about what he did? Without talking about how he left her apartment in Florida that day just two weeks before her graduation?

"Yes, I want to talk about the wedding," Adan confirmed. "What else would I want to talk to you about?"

Zena rolled her eyes.

"Look, what about the wedding? What do you want to talk about? That it's stupid? That these two have no grounds to get married? That they'll be divorced in two years? That you're wasting your money on this dress and God only knows why?" Zena listed. "Because if those aren't the key points of your conversation, I don't know what else there is for us to say to each other."

"Why shouldn't they get married?"

"Because we're a mess. Because we're not ready."

"We?"

"What?" Zena was confused.

"You said, 'we,'" Adan pointed out.

"I said *they.*"

"Well, I disagree. I think they're ready. As a matter of fact, I was the one who told Alton to propose."

"You've got to be joking. You planted this seed?" Zena snarled.

"Yes. I think it will be good for Alton. Give him a little motivation. He loves Zola. He'll do anything for her—you know that. Maybe having a family will help him focus on his dreams," Adan explained.

"Focus? What about Zola's focus? What about her dreams? She's not ready for a family. She was just about to take the Bar. Do you know she's not taking it now? Not taking it because of this wedding?" Zena asked. "Wait! Was that your idea, too?"

"She can take it next year when they get settled," Adan said.

"She'll be pregnant by next year. And did you wait a year to take the Bar? No. You were focused.

Right, Adan?" Zena charged. "You kept your 'eyes on the prize.'"

"Where'd that come from?" Adan looked as if he hardly remembered saying that to Zena.

"It came from you. How could you possibly forget?" Tears gathering in her eyes, Zena turned and walked quickly to her car.

Chapter 4

A little after 6:00 p.m. and Zena was laying in the center of her bed, praying for sunset and sleep. She wanted nothing else to do with this day. Too many hours had been spent living in the past, and she'd convinced herself that the future would be better. Though she hadn't been to church in over a year, she was humming notes of Yolanda Adams's rendition of "This Too Shall Pass" while forcing her eyes closed and imagining her new day at sunrise. Then, she'd run five miles and meet the sun at the top of Stone Mountain. She'd get home in time to watch the news, answer all emails and voice mails, and indulge in her two-hour beautification regime before leaving the house in a perfectly tailored black suit that captured the correct ardor and acumen of her business style. She'd zip through traffic to work in her sparkling, freshly waxed Porsche—she would've stopped by the car wash on the way home from her run—to find her designated parking spot empty at the office. Malak would have anticipated her arrival and had all necessary files and information needed to have the perfect day stacked in a neat little pile ready for Zena's entry. There would be no Zola and Alton, no Mommy and no damn Adan. Everything would be back to normal, back to perfection in the morning—if only she could get there.

The bright sun outside her bedroom window sure wasn't helping. The loud rush-hour traffic buzzing past her building didn't help the situation. Neither was her praying and gospel singing. Not even the four shots of whiskey she'd downed like Kool-Aid. Nothing, in fact, was working. And the biggest setback of all: Zena's own heart. It just refused to cooperate. While her mind had the plot and plan to return to business as usual, her heart was a mess of business unfinished. And what was that? So many emotions she'd convinced herself to toss aside or bury deep down inside. So many complicated emotions she'd successfully hidden away that were now springing forth like those blooming perennials in her mother's garden. The worst thing about emotions springing forth from unfinished business of the heart was that the more Zena tried to take control, the stronger these emotions became, the louder they became, the freer, the wilder.

It was Adan's scent. How it had interrupted everything inside Lucille's Lace and had whispered something to Zena she couldn't understand or recall? And it wasn't his cologne or his aftershave. It was his real scent. The actual scent of him. The one she knew. The one she'd inhaled through so many nights and woken up to on so many mornings. It was his aura. His entire being collected in free aromatic notes set for olfactory seduction. And that was it. Straight seduction. After all these years, Adan had walked into Lucille's Lace and seduced her with his scent. How could she have been so stupid? Have fallen for this trick? It was a trick, right? Why hadn't she covered her nose? Held her breath? Pulled one of those gas masks soldiers wore in those World War II movies out of her purse and run for cover the moment Adan walked into the store?

But, no, it wasn't seduction. *Seduction* would mean she'd been *seduced*. That she'd fallen for the trick. That Zena wanted Adan. That Zena wanted anything from Adan. And she didn't. Right?

Zena denied response to this internal debate, but it reminded her of her first big blowup with Adan, the one that nearly tore them apart. The two were still head over heels and happily living in the land of puppy love. But, still, Zena had been feeling as if there was a change in her first real boyfriend. They'd been together five months and kept a pretty regular schedule: any waking moment when they weren't otherwise busy, they were with each other. Their relationship was equally a close friendship and a romance, and so hours together were heartwarming and sweet but also easy and comfortable. When she was with Adan, Zena felt as complete as she could possibly be. It was as if Adan was a part of her, a gateway into her conscious, her thoughts and feelings.

That was why when Adan canceled four hangout dates in a row, Zena became suspicious. Well, her feelings didn't begin with suspicion. First she was simply off put by his announcement that he wouldn't be able to take her to their normal Saturday-morning matinee movie when Zena's mother was home from work and she didn't have to watch Zola. They'd been going to see movies each Saturday morning for eight weeks, so it was different but not unimaginable that Adan wanted to miss one day. It gave Zena pause, but she kept it inside and stayed in bed that Saturday.

The next weekend, Adan canceled the movie date and backed out of the roller-skating rink with Zena and the rest of their friends from school. Zena went alone but felt so lonely without Adan, she sat quietly throughout most of the night and went home early. When Malak and her boyfriend dropped Zena off, she stopped at the top of the walkway to her house and looked down at Adan's house with sad eyes. Forlorn and a little curious, Zena thought to run to Adan's house and bang on the door, ordering that he tell her what was going on. After all, he didn't even have a reason for canceling all of these times. He kept saying he was tired or studying. But that was all. Zena decided against running down the street and cornering Adan. She didn't want to seem like some jealous and insecure girlfriend who couldn't ever leave her boyfriend alone even to study or sleep.

But then the last straw was a week before her sixteenth birthday. Everyone was heading to the Civic Center downtown to see Goodie Mob, Adan's all-time favorite group in the world. The day before the show, though, Adan announced that yet again, he couldn't go, because he had to study. Standing beside Adan's locker as he got his books together for his next class, Zena scoffed and turned to stomp away from Adan in disgust.

"Wait! What's wrong?" Adan asked, grabbing her arm to stop her.

"Study? Yeah, right. Study what? I'm in all of your classes, and we don't have any tests coming up."

Adan frowned as if Zena was being irrational,

and Zena hated that. "I don't only study for exams. I study to be intelligent," he said.

"Well, go right on ahead. You be intelligent," Zena snapped back.

"What?" Adan pushed.

"You love Goodie Mob! Why would you miss their concert?" Zena asked. "Look, are you seeing some other girl? Is that it? Do you want to break up?" The words from Zena's mouth released some emotional torrent inside of her. She didn't even know where it came from, but she started crying and shaking and saying things to Adan that she didn't even mean. Some other kids in the hallway started looking on, so Adan quickly pulled Zena into the classroom beside his locker.

The room was empty and dark. Zena walked over to the window and wrapped her arms around her waist. "Adan, I can take it now. If you want to break up now, I can take it."

Adan responded with, "What are you talking about?"

Zena turned to him, looking surprised that he wasn't following. "You keep canceling dates with me. You're not talking to me. You keep saying you're studying and sleeping. So, I'm thinking you just want to break up."

Adan still looked lost, even more confused. "No. Not at all. That's not it." He laughed a little, but quickly hid his chuckles. He walked over to

Zena beside the window. He opened her closed arms and smiled at her.

"What are you smiling about?" Zena asked.

"I'm smiling because this is funny. Because you think I want to break up with you and what I feel is the opposite," he said. "Zena, do you want to know why I've been canceling on you? Why I'm not going to the concert?" Zena nodded. Adan reached into his back pocket and pulled out his wallet. He handed it to Zena.

"What? What's this for?" she asked.

"I can show you better than I can tell you," Adan said. "Open my wallet and inside you will find $73.48. All the money I've saved for the last month."

Zena opened the wallet and counted the money. Adan knew the exact amount. "So? Why is that important?" she asked him.

"It's the money I've been saving to take you out someplace nice for your birthday. I asked my father for money, but he said it was important that I saved my own money to take you out. That's what a man should do. That's why we haven't been going to the movies and I couldn't go skating or to see Goodie Mob—because I want to take you out to a nice dinner for your birthday. Can't you see? I don't want to break up with you. I want to be with you. I love you."

Struggling to erase this sweet memory of the

first time Adan said he loved her, Zena was rolling around in her bed like a toddler in the middle of a tantrum. Soon, she gave up on sleep and reached for her cell phone. Thankfully, Adan's number was not in her phone book, because right then he would've gotten a confusing, whiskey-tinged earful about how he'd lied to her that day in the empty classroom.

Instead of phoning her ex with a drunken diatribe, naturally, Zena called her best friend.

"You told that man where I was?" Zena blurted out when Malak answered.

"Hum. I guess this means you saw Adan?" Malak posed the question coolly. "And judging from your voice, you've seen Jack Daniel's, too. I thought it would take you at least a week to turn to the bottle. But I see it's been what—like eight hours?— and you're already giving me Diana Ross in *Mahogany* over the phone. Do you need me to come over there?"

"No!" Zena protested, poking out her lip as if Malak could see it. But her protest wasn't quite convincing. She needed her best friend with her. She knew it and Malak knew it.

As if she'd heard the opposite, Malak replied, "Okay. I'll be there in like two hours. I need to get the kids and drop them at my mama's. And don't drink all the liquor, either. I want some."

Zena hung up and covered her face with the first

thing she could grasp—some lumpy red throw pillow she kept reminding herself to throw out. The simple satin square matched nothing in her stark taupe and ecru bedroom, and it mostly maintained its residency due to tradition and Zena's own forgetfulness. In fact, she'd actually forgotten where the little red pillow had come from in the first place, and that was part and parcel of her reluctance to toss it out. She remembered having the pillow on her bed at her first apartment in Daytona Beach. But she didn't remember how it had gotten there. Didn't ever remember buying it. Sometimes she imagined showing up to one of her Bethune-Cookman reunions and hearing one of her old roommates ask if anyone had the old red pillow her dead grandmother had made, or something like that. Zena would reveal that she still had the thing, and they would have a good hug before Zena produced the pillow and saved the day.

But right then as the lumpy satin pillow soaked up Zena's tears and anger, she knew this was all a figment of her imagination. As she pressed the pillow to her face, it pulled her thoughts back. That pillow didn't belong to any of her old roommates. No one's dead grandmother had made it with her bare hands. The little stupid pillow was a Kmart Bluelight Special Adan had picked out for Zena's first apartment two weeks before the start of sophomore year. He'd tossed it into her cart.

"Red? Why did you put that into the cart?" Zena stopped pushing the cart and reached to pull out the red pillow, but Adan grabbed her hand.

"Just get it. It'll look nice on your bed," Adan said.

"But my comforter is purple and tan." Zena pointed to the full-size bed-in-a-bag set in the cart. Beneath it, she had a purple lava lamp, a set of plastic purple hangers and a tan photo collage wall hanger, all decorations for Zena's bedroom in her first off-campus apartment she'd share with three other coeds.

"You need a pop of color, Z," Adan said confidently.

Zena grinned. "What do you mean 'a pop of color'? What do you know about that?"

"It's the style. All the girls at Spelman have one pop of color in their dorm rooms. Like pink and white with turquoise. Or red and black with yellow."

All summer after freshman year, Zena had to listen to Adan talking about how the Spelman girls across the street from Morehouse did this and that. How they wore their hair and what kind of music they were listening to. Adan would go on about his Spelman sister, Morenike, and her natural hair. That Morenike was going to study in Paris sophomore year and Zena should do the same thing. It would look good on her Harvard application.

"Red, black and yellow is disgusting, and how do you know what the dorm rooms at Spelman look like?" Zena asked suspiciously; she'd already decided that Adan was cheating on her and had fallen in love with Morenike.

"Because I've been in the dorm rooms at Spelman," Adan replied with not one marker of nervousness.

"Really? And what would you say if I said I'd been in the male dorms at Bethune-Cookman?" Zena pushed herself between Adan and the cart and put her hands on her hips to strengthen her inquisition.

"I'd say, 'I'm happy for you,'" Adan answered. "I'd ask what colors the guys in Daytona Beach are using to decorate their rooms."

Zena huffed and stomped to the back of the cart before tossing the red pillow back onto the shelf.

"Really? Don't do the jealous thing, Z. You're so much cooler when you're confident."

"I am confident, but I don't care how the girls at Spelman decorate their rooms, and I definitely don't want to hear about it or that you're all up in their rooms."

"Why not? The only reason you wouldn't want to hear it is if you think I'm cheating with one of them."

"Are you?"

"Hell no!"

"Then why are you always talking about them?"

"Because they're great girls—great women. And they're my friends. Why not? You want me to talk about dudes all the time?" Adan asked.

Zena said, "I want you to talk about me."

"About you? You want me to talk about you?" Adan smiled and walked toward Zena. He pushed the cart away and stood in front of her. "You know, it's funny that you complain about me talking about all those girls because all those girls complain about me talking about one girl."

"Who?"

"You," Adan revealed. "They complain because I'm always talking about how you have straight As. And how you got the Presidential Scholarship. And that you're the first in your family to go to college, but they'd never know it because you're taking junior-level classes and acing them all. And that you're so pretty. And while the girls at Spelman are cute, really cute, none of them are as beautiful as you. Not even close."

Zena was blushing and feeling stupid about arguing over the red pillow. She was about to apologize, but Adan stopped her.

"I'm not going anywhere," he said. "I know everyone keeps telling us this long-distance relationship thing doesn't work, but we're going to show them all. We're going to make it. We have a plan, and no girl at Spelman, not even my Spelman sister, is going to ruin that. I love you, Z."

The Bluelight Special red pillow made it back into the cart and through checkout. Adan was right. It added the perfect pop of color to the purple and tan Kmart bed-in-a-bag.

By the time Malak made her way to the apartment, Zena had cut the little red pillow into so many pieces it looked as if rose petals and cotton balls were scattered all over her bedroom floor. Zena was sitting on the floor in the middle of the mess, looking as if she was trying to figure something out.

"I see you finished the liquor," Malak said, looking at the empty bottle of Honey Jack on Zena's nightstand. "How many times do I need to tell you that you can't drink?"

Malak dropped her purse and jacket on the bed and went to gather her friend off the floor.

"Let's get you back into bed," Malak said, pulling up a reluctant Zena.

Zena groaned something that sounded as if it might be a cry or helpless whimper as she allowed her friend to move her body.

"How did you get in here?" she asked Malak.

"I'm your assistant. I have a key."

Zena nodded and slid into her normal place in

the bed. Malak hopped in beside her. She reached for her purse.

"I didn't know what you had, so I made this a BYOB party." She pulled out a bottle of Hennessy. "No sense in just one of us being drunk." She giggled and slid the bottle onto the nightstand so she could go to the kitchen to get one glass.

When she returned, Zena had already opened the bottle and was taking sips through tears.

"Oh, shit!" Malak climbed onto the bed and grabbed the bottle. "You're turning down epic breakdown lane right now! I'll go with you, but you have to let me catch up." Malak poured her glass, took a quick shot and poured more Hennessy before putting the bottle back into her bag and zipping it shut. She took a sip and lay back on the pillow adjacent to Zena.

The friends rested in silence for a while, letting the moment catch up to Zena's racing emotions and Malak's alcohol level.

"I was fine," Zena whispered. "Doing just fine. I was over him. I'd moved on."

"Chile, wasn't nothing fine about you. Yes, you were doing something that looked like moving on. But wasn't nothing fine."

"I'm a successful attorney. I make a good salary. I vacation in Tahiti. I have perfect credit. I own a horse," Zena listed, struggling so hard to sound sober.

"And you don't have a man. Not-a-one!" Malak countered. "When was the last time you had a man? I sure can't remember."

Zena tried to recall this information herself; it was hard, but after some seconds she resurrected a name: "Corey! That was my last boyfriend."

"The dude with the perm? The one everybody said was gay?"

"He didn't have a perm! He was half-Panamanian. And he wasn't gay."

"You can keep claiming that, but he was gay as hell. Evidenced by the fact that he didn't ever want to get into bed with you," Malak said laughing.

"He was a Christian man who was saving it for marriage." Zena felt herself smile a little.

"No, he was saving his down-low lifestyle for marriage. As soon as you two crossed that threshold and he got those papers, you wouldn't have seen an ounce of affection for the rest of your life! Next!"

"Well…" Zena tried to recall another ex, and this required so much thought she was frowning and furrowing her brow as if she was considering some complex mathematical equation. "What about Obinna?"

"That fine African doctor?" Malak recalled. "He was a good catch. What ever happened to him?"

"He wanted me to move to Nigeria with him."

"Hell no! They get you there and it's *Not Without My Daughter* starring Zena Nefertiti Shaw as Sally Field. Next!"

Zena started frowning and furrowing again, trying to find another name, but the struggle was too difficult.

"You know what—just let it go," Malak said, "because you've already proven my point—ever since your breakup with Adan all you do is date these men who aren't available to you, or you aren't available to them. It's like you're waiting on someone or something to happen. Like you're waiting on this perfect man to show up, but we both know he doesn't exist so maybe you're waiting on a specific perfect man to show up."

"I'm not waiting on anyone. Especially not Adan."

"Then why aren't you married? Why haven't you found anyone yet, Z?" Malak asked.

"I could ask you the same thing. Why aren't you married? Why haven't you found anyone?" Zena countered.

"Because I've been married and it didn't work out. Marriage is a gamble. My ex was way too controlling. But we aren't talking about me. We're talking about you, Zena, and your lack of an ability to find a mate."

"You say it like there's something wrong with me," Zena complained.

"Because there is," Malak said flatly.

"But you just said marriage is a gamble, so how is there something wrong with me if I'm not married? That's the same crap everyone says to successful, independent black women like me! Maybe there's nothing wrong with us. Maybe we're just smarter."

"Look, I don't know about all that stuff you done read in some *Essence* 'Single in the City' article, but I know you. I'm your girl and I've been studying you more than half my life. I know what's wrong with you and when something is wrong with you. And I know exactly how you must've felt when you saw Adan today at the dress shop. And I know it broke your heart."

Zena rolled over to snuggle in Malak's arms and let her tears fall.

"That's it, girl! Let it out! Let it all out!" Malak said, patting Zena on the back.

The sun had finally set and the room was dim. Blue lights twinkled from electronic devices. Some sad Sade song should've been playing on the radio.

"What happened that night you and Adan broke up in Daytona Beach?" Malak asked. "I always wanted to know, but you never said anything. You just said it was over with him, and then you left for law school. When you came back, you made me pinkie promise never to say his name again. So I didn't, but I always wanted to."

Zena looked at the pieces of the red satin pillow all over her bedroom floor. The breakup was two weeks before graduation. She was on her third apartment by then. She only had one roommate. The red pillow was still in tow. Adan was giving his philosophical "Eyes on the Prize" speech and had broken up with her before she even realized what was happening. Again, she remembered him saying, "So, we should just be friends" in that fake, nasal "Man of Morehouse" accent he'd picked up on the debate team.

Those words sent Zena into a rage that frightened both her and Adan.

She had jumped up from the kitchen table and started wailing at him, calling him names and sobbing so deeply she wouldn't be able to stop long after she'd pushed Adan out onto the street without his car keys or his bags or anything and refused to let him back in until he returned with police.

Zena had tried to forget but still remembered all the things she'd said to Adan before she kicked him out—that she always knew he'd do this to her; he was just a liar. He was just like her father. No good. She struggled to slap him, to scratch him, to punch him, but Adan just held Zena down and told her she'd get over this—that she'd be okay without him. That only further infuriated Zena and sent her to a place beyond rage—to pure sorrow, to a real mourning over all of the love Zena had lost in her life that made her knees weak and delivered her to the floor, where Adan knelt down and tried to understand as she wept.

When it seemed as if she was almost calm, Adan had asked what she wanted him to do. How he could make things right?

Zena had cried, "Marry me. Let's get married. Then we'll move to Boston together and you can finish law school and I'll just go to school for paralegal or something. I can be your secretary. Whatever. I don't care, as long as we're together. I don't want to lose you. I can't!"

Adan had stroked Zena's hair into place. "No, we can't," he said as earnestly as he could. "I can't let you do that."

Zena had asked, "Why? Why can't you?"

"Because I believe in you too much to do that to you. And that's why I'm doing this. That's why we're breaking up. If we stay together, you'll lose yourself. Lose your dreams. And you losing your dreams, well, that's not a part of my dream," Adan had replied.

Zena found the last strength left in her knees and arms to get up and push Adan out the door.

"Malak, I asked that man to marry me," Zena said, remembering the confused look on Adan's face when she'd said it. "And he said he couldn't do it because he wanted us to keep sight of our dreams that apparently didn't include each other."

"That's messed up, Z," Malak said.

"It's beyond messed up. And every time I remember it, all I can think is that he was the first man I ever trusted, the first one I loved, and look at what he did. Look how he handled it. And now here he is back in Atlanta talking about how he encouraged his brother to propose to my sister, saying it will be good for them. If that isn't freaking irony? He has no problem taking my sister's eyes *off* the prize, paying for our dresses and God knows what else."

"He bought her dress?"

Zena ignored this. She popped up and looked around the dark room through newly puffy eyes. She leaned over and flicked on her bedside lamp.

"You know, the more I think about it, the more this thing just doesn't make sense," she said.

"What?" Malak sat up slowly and went for a sip of her Hennessy.

"Why is he so game to support this wedding? Is it because his own marriage failed?"

"Well, technically he was never married, so his marriage couldn't fail," Malak explained.

"You know what I mean, Malak. Maybe this is about his marriage failing to even exist and me doing perfectly fine without him," Zena said, adding up details. "I'm saying I made it! I made something of myself. I handled my part of Law: From A to Z. My *own* agency Z. Shaw Law is blowing up, and he knows it. And he knows that I also managed to pull my little sister up and make something of her—something he's only halfway done with Alton, the wannabe neo-soul singer. So now he wants to bring me down."

Malak squinted as she tried to arrive at Zena's conclusions. "Nah. Sounds kinda crazy to me."

Zena jumped up from the bed with her thoughts racing to epiphany.

"I'm not going to let him do this," she announced.

"Do what?"

"Ruin what I've worked so hard for, so he can just placate his own male ego!"

"I don't know what any of that means," Malak confessed, rubbing her forehead.

"It means—I can't let this wedding happen. I can't let Adan win. Can't you see it, Malak? If those two get married, the same thing Adan was so afraid was going to happen to me will happen to Zola. She'll be living in Alton's shadow forever. She'll never live her dream."

"The dream you gave her?" Malak pointed out.

Zena rolled her eyes. She stood before her bedroom window watching traffic roll up Peachtree Road toward Buckhead.

Malak was behind her, saying something about

Zola being in love and Zena needing to support it no matter what, but Zena was already caught up in her thoughts and heard little of the speech.

"I'm not going to let him do this," Zena repeated. "I can't."

Part II

Under the Bali Moon

Chapter 5

Zena got Adan's telephone number from a thoroughly surprised Zola and called him to apologize for her behavior outside Lucille's Lace. She chuckled coyly and claimed she hoped he'd accept her apology for being so reckless with her words. Adan sounded just as surprised as Zola, but he accepted Zena's apology and matched it with one of his own. He hadn't meant to upset her or anyone else. He explained that he simply wanted to "do what is right for Alton and Zola."

Zena gushed at his greatness and agreed to do the same. She revealed that she was so happy Zola was marrying Alton. And she'd decided she was going to Bali. She had to be by her baby sister's side. "Really?" Adan asked.

"Of course! What? Do you think I would lie about something like that?"

Adan should've said, "yes," of course, because Zena was definitely lying. Zena's saccharine-laced approval of Adan's support of the wedding and her sudden decision to be there to play the loving and devoted big sister were a meticulously orchestrated oral camouflaging set to conceal what Zena really had going on.

At the top of a long list of things Zena knew about Zola were two important facts she'd forgotten in recent days:

Zola thrived on love and trust.

Zola especially thrived on love and trust from Zena.

There were times during their childhood when Zena and Zola were just simply attached at the hip. And not because they were sisters; it was because with everything going on around them—Daddy cheating and making more babies with more women; Mommy struggling just to feed them and keep a roof over their heads—Zena and Zola only had each other to depend on.

They couldn't go to their father with their problems—half the time they didn't even know where he lived. They couldn't go to their mother with their problems—sometimes when she got home from working doubles in the catering department at Delta Air Lines, her feet would be so swollen all she wanted to do was lie on the couch in absolute silence.

The girls went to each other then; they leaned on each other. First periods. First dances. First boyfriends. First broken hearts. They trusted each other through it all. And even when Zena outgrew this full dependence on Zola, the little sister kept her focus and leaned on the big sister. And she never really stopped. Zola loved and trusted Zena more than anyone in the world—Malak had been right about that.

Once, when Zola was four and they were still living in the projects in Queens, she claimed there was a ghost under the bed. Zena, ten years old and left alone to take care of her little sister, pretended she believed Zola and asked Zola to show her the ghost. They crept out of the bed and got down on their knees and peeled back the sheet hanging over the bed. Zola was so nervous, she kept her little eyes squinted in fear of actually seeing something scary. Zena told her to point out the ghost. Zola peeked. Zena begged to see the ghost. Zola opened one eye. Zena asked where the ghost was. Zola opened her second eye. Soon, Zola was looking wide-eyed at her fears. "See, no ghost," Zena said, smiling. "No ghost here. No ghost anywhere."

If Zena wanted Zola to see that getting married

was going to set her back and potentially ruin everything she'd worked so hard for, she couldn't keep throwing it all in Zola's face. She couldn't keep telling Zola everything that was going wrong. She had to let Zola see things for herself. She had to let Zola get out of the bed, get on her knees and peek under the bed to find her own ghosts. And just as she did when they were little, she had to be by Zola's side.

"Zollie Rollie Polie!" Zena was standing in the lobby of Hartsfield-Jackson Airport with one arm open and ready to receive a hug from her sister. A huge black luggage roller was at her feet.

"Zollie?" Zola laughed, hugging Zena. "You haven't called me that in like years." She had her own luggage roller at her feet. It was hot pink and bigger than Zena's, and the word *Bride* was stitched on the front pocket in white.

Two weeks had passed, and after successfully showering her sister in sugary speeches and all the comforts any bride could desire, including a small spa shower the day before the Bali departure, Zena was officially a maid of honor to-be.

She arrived at the airport with her game face hidden beneath black shades and a surprise behind her back.

"Come on, how could I forget your nickname?" Zena joked with Zola before revealing her surprise. "And how could I forget how you got that old nickname?"

In her right hand, Zena was balancing a huge box of Krispy Kreme doughnuts she'd picked up on the way to the airport.

"You remembered?" Zola laughed. "I can't believe you remembered!"

"How could I forget? Like the one thing you loved when we moved to Atlanta was these damn Krispy Kreme doughnuts. You loved them so much, you got a little gut, and me and Mommy started calling you—"

Zola cut in with "Zollie Rollie Polie!"

The sister's laughed together at the memory of Zola going completely insane every time she saw that dark orange Hot Now sign lit up when they passed the old Krispy Kreme window on Abernathy in the West End. One day, Lisa pulled over and bought Zola an entire dozen of the sticky and doughy sweets and told her to eat them all so she could get over her infatuation. It didn't work. Zola's love affair grew and grew, and soon, so did her stomach.

"I figured we could eat these before we board the plane, so we can get a little rest," Zena said.

"Rest? After we eat these doughnuts, we'll be bouncing off the walls!"

"Not once we get on the plane and have a little bit of that free wine!"

"The *free* international-flight wine!" Zola recalled, reaching for the doughnuts.

"Exactly."

Zola and Zena tore through six Krispy Kreme doughnuts apiece—a small victory for anyone familiar with the addictive brand. They rushed toward their flight, and once aboard they celebrated Zola's coming new life with so many wine toasts they were both asleep within an hour.

It was still a long fifteen hours in the air before their layover in Korea. Zola and Zena kept each other company by telling stories and making plans. There were baby names and shared vacations. There were decisions about what religion Zola would practice in her new home—if any. Would she and Alton become full vegans as they'd planned? Would they raise vegan babies? Zena grimaced at the thought of any child eating soy crumbles all their life.

While Zena wasn't exactly excited to chat with Zola about these things, the subjects kept her from bringing up one of the things she promised she'd leave on the back burner until she got everything sorted out with Zola—the real future Zena was going to make sure Zola actually lived. The one where she was an attorney.

When they boarded the plane from Korea to Indonesia, frequent naps and in-flight movies filled the lull in the conversation between Zena and Zola.

Once, Zena looked over at Zola sitting beside the window in the first-class seats Zena reserved for their daylong journey. She found Zola looking off into the clouds, smiling at nothing. She imagined Zola must've been thinking about Alton waiting for her in Bali, setting things up for their big day.

Right then, Zena felt an arresting solitude that caught her completely off guard. There was no love she could see in the clouds. No face staring back at her. No future to project. It was just her. And what did she have? Her business? Her success? Her money? She could take care of herself. She could buy anything she wanted. Go anywhere she dreamed. But she was alone. She was worse than alone—she was lonely.

A stewardess seemed to show up from nowhere with a glass of merlot. She was an Asian woman with beautiful full lips and a wide nose that reminded Zena of some of the Melanesian women she'd met during her last vacation to Vanuatu.

Similar to her other trips to parts of Asia and throughout the Pacific, Zena noticed that when she and Zora transferred flights in Korea, most everyone on the flight was Asian; however, the diversity in complexion and hair texture and facial features was wide-ranging and similar to differences she saw between white and black people in America.

"These long flights can get to you," the stewardess said, handing the full wineglass over to Zena.

"Thank you," Zena replied.

She took a few sips of wine and looked out into the dusky night with Zola.

Adan had asked to see her a few days before they left for Bali. Actually, Adan asked to see Zena a few times. He'd called randomly. Sometimes in the middle of the night. Sometimes text. Sometimes email. He was sounding like a friend. An old friend who wanted to catch up. "I just want to see how things are with you," he'd said once when Zena actually picked up the phone to hear one of his lunch proposals.

Zena was always too busy. She was pleasant, cheery sounding, but too busy to see Adan.

What was there to see? What was there to talk about? She couldn't live in a world where she talked about how "things are" with her without screaming about how things had been with her—about how things had been with them. And even still, she didn't want to scream about how things had been with her or them. What would be the point? Why open that door? Adan was the one who'd closed the door and walked away. She was left on the inside, and she'd made herself comfortable; she'd found her own pleasure. She wasn't ready to open up and let him back in.

The villa Alton and Zola rented for the week they'd be in Bali was less than an hour from the airport. Mahatma House was a sprawling five-bedroom architectural beauty set in the middle of a lush beachfront garden.

When Zena and Zola climbed out of the disheveled minivan charged with transporting them from the airport to the villa, both tongues were wagging. Everything was gorgeous. Everything was lovely. Everything was every hyperbolic adjective they could recall: *magnificent, wondrous, amazing*! But none of their words could capture what they really saw.

From the airport to the drop-off at Mahatma House, their first impression of the Southeast Asian paradise known as Bali was a racket of beauties that made a mess of their five senses. Streets filled with dogs and motorbikes carrying men, women and children, sometimes entire families all at once. Horns beeping. Lights flashing. Red and purple and yellow flags hanging. Outdoor restaurants roasting pigs on front-yard spits. The beach. Rolling waves, black sand. Someone playing hip-hop. Another person singing a Balinese love song. Pigskin popping over the fire. Flowers blooming. Women walking the roads dressed in elaborate saris and carrying bright floral offerings to the temple. Street signs pointing in every direction. The heat—stifling and arresting.

And they'd only been there an hour.

"Where have you brought me!" Zola hollered

when she spotted Alton strumming his guitar by the pool in the central atrium at Mahatma House.

He tossed the guitar to the ground as if he couldn't care if it broke or flew away and ran to his bride.

"It's beautiful—isn't it, baby?" he said, picking Zola up and spinning her around.

"More than I could've dreamed. So much more," she answered in his arms.

Alton's countenance had far surpassed his boyish oddities. While Zena often questioned his neo-soul singing skills, there was no doubt he looked like a neo-soul star. He had big, brown pouty eyes, natural muscles and a head of auburn dreads that looked more like wild coils. He was always singing or humming something sensual and went nowhere without his beloved acoustic guitar.

Surrounded by the waitstaff in the open-air living room overlooking the pool, Zena looked on awkwardly at Zola and Alton's romantic reuniting. She smiled with pursed lips and unconsciously crossed her arms so she didn't look as if she was expecting anyone to greet her with open arms.

"Uhhh, Mister Adan, he come now for you," one of the housekeepers said to Zena.

"No, no, no," Zena said, and nervously sputtered out, "He's not for me. He's my childhood friend. We aren't together. He's just a family friend. I don't like him or anything."

The housekeeper nodded at her, though it was obvious she wasn't following along with the elaborate explanation of why a thirty-something woman was standing alone in the lobby of one of the most romantic villas in one of the most romantic places in the world.

"You guys are here!" Zena heard.

She turned to see Adan descending a set of black polished-concrete stairs that led to one of the bedrooms in the main house, where she was standing.

"Yes, we are," she said.

Adan walked over to Zena and hugged her. Over his shoulder, Zena saw the housekeeper smiling at her knowingly.

"How were your travels?" Adan asked, releasing Zena a bit but not letting her out of his arms. He kind of rested them on her waist and leaned back to look at her.

"Safe?" Zena answered, stepping back to escape his embrace.

"Good to hear you were safe." Adan nodded.

The night moon brought a delicious Balinese feast spread out on a long wooden table overlooking the black sand beach at Mahatma House. Dressed in all white, as requested by the house concierge, Alton and Zola, Adan and Zena arrived at their welcoming dinner to drink in a cornucopia of traditional culinary delights. Prawns as big as the men's fists, nutty chicken satay right off the grill, sweet and spicy tempeh, and at the center of the table was the *babi guling*, a suckling pig that had been roasting in the yard most of the day.

The ocean breeze rolled up the strand, mixed with the food and tantalized all at the table.

"I hope they don't think we're going to eat all of this," Zola said, looking over the foreign delicacies. "Look at all of this meat! And is this a baby pig? Yuck!"

"Well, if you don't eat your portion, I'll gladly take it," Zena offered, sitting beside her. She'd seen Alton hungrily eyeing the porker since they'd sat at the table, and she remembered Zola pondering his going vegan with her on the plane.

"Now, that's what I'm talking about! Let's get our grub on!" Alton said before giving Zena a high five from the opposite side of the table where he was sitting beside Adan.

"So you're eating everything on the table—even the meat?" Zola pointed to the steamy *babi guling* with the traditional apple stuffed into its mouth.

"Darling, we're in paradise. I don't think vegan rules apply," Alton joked. "Besides, we're not Muslim. A little pig never hurt nobody."

"Not *that* little pig, anyway. I'm pretty sure it hasn't hurt anybody," Adan said, fixated on the baby pig as he rubbed his stomach. "What, you think that porker is like two weeks old?" He leaned over to Alton and laughed.

"I don't know, but I bet he tastes good!" Alton replied, and both of the house waiters standing guard beside the table chuckled but then went back to their serious on-duty stances.

"I can't believe what I'm hearing! You guys are totally gross!" Zola complained.

"Okay! Okay! Okay! I'm totally sorry for grossing you out, future baby sister," Adan said. He picked up a spoon and tapped at his glass, making a clatter. "Hear ye! Hear ye!" he began. "Now, if I may have your attention for a moment please. I need to make some announcements."

Zena had taken in all of Adan in his loose-fitting white linen Havana shirt and trousers. He and Alton had only gotten to Bali two days before she'd arrived with Zola, but both men already had sufficient tans. Adan's brown skin was a smooth pumpernickel now, and the white linen made his arms and face look like something to touch. She made sure to look away as he spoke. She spotted two dogs chasing waves a mile or so down the beach. No owner in sight, no people around at all; however, they still appeared to enjoy a kind of human fun on a beauteous evening between the black sky and black sand.

"First, I want to say I'm so happy we are all to-gether," Adan went on in her ear. "I'm so happy to share this amazing occasion with so many amazing—"

Zena looked out to the ocean as Adan continued his welcoming. There, she focused on one ship floating so far out she could only see its navigation lights meant to both confirm and reveal its location as it floated through the night.

"You know what? Let's stop this right now?" Zena curtly interrupted Adan.

Everyone looked at Zena nervously, as if they'd been waiting for her to say something out of line or do something outrageous.

"What? What is it, Zena? Everything okay?" Zola asked carefully as she reached over and placed a calming hand on Zena's knee.

"Yes, silly. I'm just saying—let's stop all this welcoming stuff," she said, adding more cheerfulness to her tone. "In fact, Adan shouldn't be the one welcoming us all here anyway."

"Who should be welcoming us, Zena?" Alton asked, and at that moment he sounded as though he fully expected the people from the local crazy house to show up to take Zena away in a straitjacket and human muzzle.

"You!" Zena said. "You two. The bride and groom should be opening the wedding weekend with a welcoming for their guests." Zena looked to Adan for support. "I'm guessing you and I have been to the same amount of weddings. Am I correct? Isn't that how it goes?"

"Yes," Adan confirmed.

"Oh," Zola uttered, as if none of that had occurred to her, though Zena knew she'd been to and even participated in a few of her line sisters' weddings. "So, that's cool." Zola looked at Alton, who appeared just as surprised and also speechless. "Well," she giggled girlishly. "I guess, we both say, 'Welcome?'"

Alton nodded as if his betrothed had really done something, and he cavalierly repeated, "Yeah. Welcome," before easing back in his seat comfortably.

Even Adan looked perturbed by this nonchalance.

"Come on! You guys have to do better than that," Zena pointed out. "You sound like teenagers. This is your wedding. The most adult thing you could do. You have to do better."

"It's not that we don't want to do better. We just don't know what to say," Zola complained.

"Okay! Okay! Well, in the interest of time, and so our lovely food doesn't go untouched for too much longer, I'll give a suggestion," Zena offered. "How about you two stand and welcome Adan and me here. And then share something special with us. Say…" Zena looked around and snapped her fingers as if she was trying to find a solution, but the truth was that she'd planned this—she'd already used her interrogation skills to come up with the perfect prompts to cause contention between Alton and Zola. "You could ummm… I have it… You could tell your guests what you see in each other. Why you believe your mate would make a good husband or wife."

Adan nodded at the suggestion and looked at Alton and Zola, who started getting up rather awkwardly like two teens about to give a speech before their classmates.

"Welc—" Zola tried, but Zena quickly stopped her.

"No, Alton should start," Zena demanded. "He's the man. The husband. He speaks for both of you… now."

Adan nodded again, though he also looked as if this might have been a quizzical detail for someone like Zena, who only ever let him speak first when she had nothing to say when they were children.

"Well, it's the twenty-first century, and I don't see my soon-to-be wife as a second-class citizen," Alton said sarcastically. "She's my equal. My soul mate. But I'll play along." He cleared his throat and shook away his nervousness. "Welcome, everyone. My lovely bride and I are so happy to have you here this evening as we prepare for our nuptials. I *believeith* it was the good *brotherith* Common who *saidith*, 'It don't take all day to recognize sunshine,'" he went on in jest. "Well, I did recognize that sunshine in this badass chick beside me, and I'm never letting her put me in the dark again."

Zena was staring at Alton and struggling to hide her frown of displeasure at the cute but out-of-place Common rap song quote. "And tell us, beyond being *sunshine*—because we all know that about Zola—what will make her a good wife?"

Alton bit his upper lip as he contemplated. A bright light from one of the tiki torches set up around the table sparkled behind him. Soon, he said, "She's a good person. She's nice. She's nice to me. And she's beautiful. And I love her."

Zola swooned and leaned into Alton. "So sweet," she said.

Zena smiled weakly and turned her attention to Zola. "And you—why do you believe Alton will make a good husband?"

Zola grinned at Alton, and she had to hold the grin for a long while because it took her twice as long as it had taken Alton to gather a response. So long, in fact, that one of the staffers beside the table seemed to lean in with anticipation.

Soon, Zola spoke to Alton as if they were alone. "Alton, you are comforting. You are so fine!" She smiled. "You are always sweet. You love me. You're a good man."

"Oh, babe!" Alton said.

One of the staff members wiped a loose tear-drop as Alton kissed Zola.

Clearly unimpressed, Zena started a slow clap until Alton and Zola stopped kissing, and she offered a well-intentioned smile.

"That's sweet," she said. "Very sweet. And so original. No at all what I expected. I've heard so many brides and grooms respond to that very question and they say things like, 'She's good with money and children and has good credit and is godly,' and 'He's stable and successful and intelligent and ambitious.' Those are the kinds of answers I'm used to hearing, but I think what you two said was sufficient. It was well-meaning. It was beautiful. Right, Adan?" Her tone was indicting and a little sarcastic, but not blatantly attacking. She didn't want to cause alarm.

Adan had clearly caught on to something, though, and was staring at Zena, trying to discover her point.

"Right, Zena. You're right," he concurred.

Bellies filled with so much rice and pork—even Zola had eaten her share—and everything else at the table, the foursome ambled to their rooms to shut it down for the night. Though they'd chatted about an evening stroll on the beach and even planned a midnight pool party, the days of travel, gross sensual demands of the new environment, good eating and the ocean breeze around them had everyone feeling completely exhausted or so thoroughly relaxed they could fall asleep at any moment.

While Zola, who announced that she didn't want to sleep with Alton so she could be "chaste" before the wedding, had her own room in the main house, she opted to share a bed with Zena in the flat she'd selected toward the back of the property. The simple architectural offering was elegant and mysterious. Four walls of cool black polished concrete came together to create a kind of human-sized cocoon made for perfect sleeping.

When Zena got out of the shower, she found Zola sitting on the edge of the king-size bed wrapped in a towel. Zola's hair was completely covered with leave-in conditioner. She'd split it into four sections and was busy twisting.

"What are you going to do with your hair for the wedding?" Zena asked. She was naked and standing before the vanity a few feet away from the bed. She'd discovered two mosquito bites on her arm and was dutifully applying Skin So Soft, a bite repellant and remedy Lisa had passed down to her daughters.

"I don't know. I was thinking you could corn-row it up into a goddess knot or something. Like how you used to do when I was younger."

"I don't think my braiding skills are wedding day worthy," Zena said.

"I don't think I have a choice."

"Ahhh. The black-woman travel dilemma," Zena confirmed, laughing. "No one to do your hair."

"Exactly."

"You never know. There must be one hairdresser in all of Bali who can do braids! Some of these people here have some coarse hair!"

"Yeah, I know."

"Plenty of folks look surprised to see us, though. It's like they've never seen black people, period."

"Alton said some guy at the airport asked to take a picture with him. Can you believe that?" Zola revealed. "Then after taking the picture, the man gave him a thumbs-up and said, 'Michael Jordan!'"

"Ahhh. The black-man travel dilemma," Zena confirmed, laughing again. "Everyone thinks you're an athlete."

Zola laughed, and then the sisters were silent as she finished her third braid.

Zena brushed her teeth and looked at her hairline. She'd plucked three gray hairs. While Lisa kept telling her not to pull them out, that the aggressive action would only invite more, she just couldn't stand the sight of the white hairs.

"You hear that?" Zola said, looking at the door.

"What?"

"Listen."

Zena stopped moving and listened, but she heard nothing.

"What?"

"It's crickets." Zola smiled. "Crickets!"

Then Zena could hear them, too. It was a simple buzzing that sounded like nothing until she tuned in, and then the crickets were chirping all around.

"Night crickets. Just like in Georgia," Zola observed whimsically. "It's beautiful. We're literally on the other side of the world but still at home."

Zena slid on her nightgown and headed toward her side of the bed.

"I've been thinking about what you said," Zola started, rather abruptly changing the subject. "About the things Alton and I should have said about one another when we listed what would make a good husband or wife."

"I didn't say you should've said anything. I said what you revealed was enough."

"I know. I know," Zola agreed. "But I mean like the other things were important, too. People don't like to say it, but they are."

Zena grinned internally and asked, "Like what? What things are important?" Then she tried to sound more nonchalant and less leading with, "I don't really recall everything I said. Remind me."

"You said other people have told you their fiancé/ fiancée was good with money or had good credit."

"Finances? So you meant to say Alton is *good* with finances?" Zena asked naively.

Zola rolled her eyes at Zena. "Stop joking. You know he has no real finances to be good with. Not now anyway."

Zena nodded.

"And when he does get money, we've been so broke for so long, we just spend it because we're both so frustrated," Zola added.

"That's life with an artist." Zena sat beside Zola and reached over to twist Zola's last plait.

"But will it work?" Zola asked. "You work with people going through divorces all the time. Does it work? Like if Alton doesn't make it. If he never gets his career together."

"I'm not here to do that, Zollie," Zena said. "I told you I'm just here to support you and Alton on your special day."

"Cut the crap. Just answer the question." Zola pulled away from Zena's hold on her hair and looked at her.

"Fine." Zena groaned as if Zola had really pulled her arm and none of this was planned. "There's no right or wrong answer here. But I can say in my practice—money is most commonly at the root of divorce. That and cheating."

Zola sighed.

"Look, low cash makes everything more difficult," Zena said.

"But plenty of people with lots of cash have issues, too," Zola pointed out. "You know that."

"Low cash is an issue that can hit anyone. A rich man can have low cash issues if his wife is trying to be in a new Bentley every month. It's nothing to have $50K in the bank if your mortgage alone is $10K. If the light bill is $1,500."

"Good point," Zola said. "You know, Alton is talking about getting a house for us."

"Really?" Zena looked shocked. "Where?"

"Mr. Roy wants to give us their old house. He's been lonely with Mrs. Pam gone, and he's moving back to his family farm in Valdosta."

"That's wonderful. What a gift for you two."

"Not really. I don't want to live in our old neighborhood. I want something nice. I want something new. I want to stay downtown."

"I could sell you guys my condo," Zena offered easily.

"You'd do that?"

"Of course. I only owe like a couple hundred thousand on the loan. How's Alton's credit?" She didn't bother to ask about Zola. Her credit was so bad, Zena was surprised Zola was deemed fit to sit for the Bar Exam.

"You owe that much? We can't afford that. How much do you pay each month for the mortgage?" Zola asked with her mouth open in surprise. "Wait! I don't think I want to know."

Zola gasped and fell back on her pillow in time to hear a rolling wave beat out the crickets.

"I have so much to think about," she declared, sounding deflated.

Zena turned off the lamp beside the bed before lying back on her pillow.

"Too late for all that," she said, openly smiling in the darkness. "No cold feet allowed on this trip. You're getting married."

Chapter 6

Zena felt so rejuvenated by the bedtime discussion with Zola that she woke up in time for sunrise, endured a five-mile jog through the homey village outside Mahatma House, showered, blew out her hair and still managed to be the first person at the breakfast table. She wore a loose-fitting yellow beach dress and slid a red hibiscus she'd plucked during her jog behind her right ear.

The house chef greeted Zena with a cup of green tea that seemed oddly comforting in the early heat that invaded the outdoor dining area. She slid a plate of sliced exotic fruit onto the table and took Zena's breakfast order.

After a while, Adan entered. He was wearing a pair of Hawaiian print blue-and-white swimming trunks and no shirt.

Zena glanced and looked away quickly. How odd was it that he wasn't wearing a shirt? How odd was it that he was there?

She counseled herself that perhaps she should've expected these two things: his presence, his nude and muscular chest.

Zena suddenly hated herself for getting to the breakfast table first. She also hated herself for not having a T-shirt for Adan in her bag.

"Morning, Z," Adan said, now standing beside Zena with his nude chest still wet from the pool.

He kissed her on the cheek and sat in the chair next to her as if he'd been doing this every morning of every day of the year.

The chef brought his green tea and took his breakfast order.

"You see Zola and Alton?" Zena asked. When she'd gotten to the room after her run, Zola wasn't in the bed. She assumed Zola slipped off to Alton's room.

"Yeah. They were arguing about something way too early this morning," Adan revealed.

"Really? About what?" Zena leaned toward Adan but then quickly masked her interest.

"No clue. I heard Zola shout 'condo' and 'credit,' and I pulled my pillow over my head."

Zena smirked and flexed her pinkie as she took the next sip from her tea.

"I also saw you running earlier. I was going to join you, but a brother is a little too slow these days." Adan rubbed his stomach playfully. Zena watched as his fingers grazed his perfect abs and held back from swooning. "All work and no working out makes Adan a fat man!"

Zena found herself laughing. Adan could be funny. He could be really funny sometimes.

"You're not fat," she said. "Not at all." Her voice let on that she'd gotten an eyeful of his body.

"Stop lying to me."

"I'm serious. You're in great shape."

"So, you think I'm sexy?" Adan teased as he moved his hands back behind his head and flexed.

"I never said anything about 'sexy.'" Zena rolled her eyes.

"Guess that's a no." Adan frowned and lowered his arms.

Laughing again, Zena realized then that she was having a conversation with Adan. She was in Bali, sitting at a table eating star fruit with her ex and having a civil conversation. And everything was okay.

"You're pushing it," Zena said sternly.

"Maybe I'm trying to push it."

Just in time, two plates of what the chef had called

"American Breakfast"—omelets, potatoes, bacon—were slid onto the table before Zena and Adan.

"No rice for you, either?" Adan asked.

"I don't get it. I can't eat rice for breakfast. Sue me!" Zena held up her hands.

"I agree. America wins this battle. All of Asia loses! I mean, rice for breakfast?"

"Do you think we should wait to eat with Alton and Zola?" Zena asked.

"Nah. They'll resurface when they want to. You know young'uns don't need breakfast," Adan joked. "And anyway, I'm glad to have you to myself—"

Zena cut Adan off with a sharp eye and a suspicious, "Why?"

Adan went on uneasily: "Because I wanted to go over today's exciting schedule with you and get some ideas from you about the wedding."

"Oh. I thought all these things would've been handled."

"Nah. I'm trying to be more fluid in my old age."

"Fluid?"

"Yeah. Look, I'm trying to figure out if the wedding should be in the little temple they have down the beach or just on the beach."

"Shouldn't that be up to Alton and Zola? Perhaps we can let them make that decision?"

"Good point. Well, do you want to read something during the ceremony? Like a poem?"

"Again, let's let them plan that," Zena said.

Adan looked surprised, as if Zena was driving a hard bargain. "I guess I just want things to be really nice for them."

"If they want things to be really nice, they're old enough to see it through. You've done enough. Hell, I've done enough. I'm just here to support them and have fun," Zena said. "Now, tell me about all the exciting things we have planned for today."

"I will. But first, I want you to answer a few things for me."

Zena didn't respond. In fact, she turned to look away from Adan. His words, his tone, made it clear that they were edging into a conversation she was avoiding.

"Why didn't you meet up with me in Atlanta?" Adan asked the back of Zena's head.

He waited a second, and when she didn't say anything, he added, "I really, really wanted to see you."

Zena exhaled and looked down at her food. "I was busy," she said softly.

"No one's that busy." Adan's voice was softer. He actually sounded hurt. "Like all day... I called you all day." He laughed uncomfortably.

Zena looked over at him. "Okay. Fine. I didn't want to see you. That's why I kept saying no."

"Why not?"

"Why does it matter?"

"It matters because I care," Adan said as Zena pretended to return to her eating. "I truly wanted to see you."

"For what? You said you wanted to meet about Alton and Zola and the wedding—well, I'm here and they're getting married. Everything is fine." Zena stuffed a forkful of scrambled egg into her mouth.

"What if I wanted more? What if I had other reasons for wanting to see you?"

His words made Zena so nervous that she felt her mind go blank. She kept stuffing her mouth with food. At some point, she stopped chewing and was just stuffing. She couldn't decipher what Adan was saying and had no idea how she could respond.

Adan didn't stop, though. His voice lowered and soft, he added, "What if I wanted to spend time with you. Like a date?"

Her mouth filled with food, Zena now knew what she wanted to say, but she couldn't. She wanted to curse and scream. To holler. A date? He had to be kidding. But eggs and bacon and fruit were in the way. Trying to struggle it all down her throat, Zena began to cough.

Adan leaned over to her and patted her back. "You okay? You okay?"

He slid his other hand onto Zena's arm to calm her. His touch sent charges through her body.

While she was choking on the food, Zena instinctively went into action, getting up and pushing Adan and his concerned face away from her.

Soon, the chef and the housekeeper were trying to help, too, but Zena held them all off with one finger pointed at Adan, demanding that he stay away. The red hibiscus had fallen from her ear as she stammered to clear the food from her throat.

Then, she felt arms weave around her waist and lift her from the floor. She tried to get free from the tightening hold, but it got tighter and tighter, forcing her stomach in and up.

Whoever was behind Zena started jerking her body up and down and telling her to breathe. In seconds, the food lodged in Zena's throat came barreling out to the floor and landed in a squishy splat.

"Uhhh!" was the collective sigh when they observed the regurgitated eggs and bacon and fruit.

The arms around Zena's waist let up, and she turned to see that it was Adan. Alton and Zola were standing next to him.

"You okay?" Zola asked.

"Yes. I'm fine," Zena said.

"Are you sure you're fine? You were choking," Adan pointed out, now looking at Zena incredulously as the chef and housekeeper, who were standing beside him, scrambled to get the vomit mess cleaned up.

"Yeah, I'm good." Zena narrowed her eyes on Adan. "Thanks."

"Guess my brother saved your life," Alton said with pride.

Zola exhaled. "I'm glad Adan was here for you. Look, we were coming to get you guys. The driver is here."

Adan scheduled Mahatma House's private chauffeur to show the foursome the best of beautiful Bali. So, through much of the morning and leading into the afternoon, Adan and Zena, Alton and Zola, sat in the back of the minivan, crisscrossing Bali's complex terrain as they visited popular and off-the-beaten-path attractions that covered massive mausoleums, dramatic sculptures, seedy swap meets and ancient rice fields that reminded them all of the roadside plantations throughout the deep South back home. While the heat outdoors might have initiated a "keep the kids indoors" weather advisory in Atlanta, crowds of Balinese workers, Australian expats, and tourists from throughout Asia and Europe packed the streets and sidewalks so tightly they seemed to contribute to the stifling conditions.

Loading in and out of the van, Zena tried most often to sit beside Zola, who had been rather quiet through most of the day. Zena could feel that something was bothering Zola, but she didn't want to force the issue and seem too concerned. Of course, she wanted to know what was going on, but she had her own issues to contend with. The word *date* had been bouncing around in her head since they left Mahatma House. More specifically, two words: *date* and *Adan*. They sounded like opposites in her thoughts, contrasting ideas that she didn't want to connect. Did Adan mean to say *date*? Was he serious? He certainly seemed serious. He did sound as if he meant it. But how could he? How could he want to date her? Why? Zena tried to pluck these questions from her thoughts, but every time she looked at Adan, or heard his voice throughout the day, they all came rushing in. And soon, *date* and *Adan* didn't sound so opposite at all. And Zena hated that.

At one of the many four-way stops where the minivan was caught in a traffic jam mosh pit of cars and mopeds and motorcycles and trucks and pedestrians and wild dogs, all seemingly going in every direction—both on- and off-road—Zena leaned into Zola and commented that even though Zola was a bad driver in Atlanta, she could be a great driver in Bali. This didn't even get a giggle out of Zola.

"Something wrong?" Zena asked.

"No. I'm just a little tired. I think the heat is getting to me," Zola confessed, and this sounded quite plausible.

They'd just left a monkey forest reserve where more than six hundred wild macaques had taken over a Hindu temple and become a real-life *Planet of the Apes* episode. While the wild and not-so-humble monkeys provided lots of laughs and camera ops, after an hour walking through the gardens, Zena and Zola had split a gallon of water in the parking lot as the foursome waited for the chauffeur to return.

Adan was sitting in the front seat beside the driver. "Well, I hope you're not too drained. We're about to hit these waves," he said, turning to face Zola and Zena. "Abdul tells me Padang Padang has the best surfing in Bali. Isn't that right, brother?" He nodded to the driver, a portly bald man with scaly dark skin that had clearly seen too many days on the beach.

"Yes, Mr. Adan. Exclusive beach in Bali. Best waves," he replied.

"Oh, I don't know. I haven't been surfing in a while, and I am kind of drained after all this sightseeing," Zena complained, still parched and a little dazed herself. The heat here added a kind of malaise that was hypnotic.

"Really? You can't be serious. Little Miss West End Swim Community Center Champ 2000 and 2001 doesn't want to surf?" Adan pressured Zena as he grinned at her.

When Adan's mother realized Zena and Zola

couldn't swim, Mrs. Pam immediately took it upon herself to see that the girls attended the free swimming classes offered at the local community center. While Zola got the hang of it quickly and became an average swimmer, Zena excelled at the sport and became competitive, going to local and state swim meets, where she usually lost but delivered a strong effort to represent their community. When Zena got to Bethune-Cookman, her love of swimming transitioned to surfing the waves at Daytona Beach. She even joined a black women's surf club, the Soul Surfing Sisters, and Adan came down to Daytona to see a few of her team's exhibitions.

Adan went on, "You came all the way to Bali, to some of the best beaches in the world, and you're not going to hit the waves the first chance you get? Some things done changed, Soul Surfing Sister!"

Zena laughed at Adan's memory, and she felt herself blushing, so she cut her laugh short.

"Well, I'm game, bro," Alton said, giving Adan a high five for his idea. He was sitting in the middle row by himself. "My love can get a few pictures of me on the board. Caption reads: Dread in the Water!" He shook his wild auburn dreadlocks as Adan laughed.

Zola hadn't. "What do you mean, 'get a few pictures'?" she asked.

"You'll be on the beach, right?" Alton said, confused. "You don't surf."

"I *have* surfed," Zola argued.

"When?" Alton asked.

"In Cancun when I went for spring break with my sorors."

"Okay," Alton acknowledged carefully. Now he was clearly sensing Zola's tension. "But this isn't some small beach in South America. This is the big time. Real waves."

"She okay," Abdul said, cutting in with his broken English. "Padang Padang good waves."

"See. I can handle it," Zola said.

"You know it's not safe for you," Alton added, concerned. "Why are you doing this?"

"If you go surfing, I'm going surfing, too," Zola replied, crossing her arms over her breasts with some newfound energy surrounding her.

Alton and Adan looked at Zena for a response, but she shook her head. She certainly didn't want to be on Adan's side.

"Don't look at me," she said. "I'm not her mama."

"But you know she's not a good swimmer," Alton argued.

"No. I know she's not the best swimmer, but she's a good swimmer. She can surf like anyone else. She can do anything she puts her mind to," Zena added.

Zola looked over at Zena with a new awareness in her eyes.

"Well, ladies," Adan resolved, wisely turning

back around to face the road ahead, "I guess we're all surfing, then."

Alton sighed and stared at Zola. "I can't believe you. You're not ready," he said.

Zola reached over and slid her hand onto Zena's lap, where no one could see. Zena felt Zola's need for warmth and covered her sister's hand with her own.

Abdul was right. The surf point at Padang Padang was like nothing Zena had seen: white sand stretching for miles against rolling waves that hit the shore unbroken and rough. Walking the strand to the surf shop, she watched bummy and new and professional surfers look out at the tide with privilege and expectation at a new wave coming in seconds. The beach was packed with sunbathers, too. Families of tourists had set up camp with beach umbrellas and coolers filled with overpriced imported beer they'd purchased from street vendors.

Zena saw how someone could spend her life out here with the sun and wind and waves. This was someone's heaven.

In the dressing room at the surf shop, Zola was struggling to get into her wet suit. She stumbled about on the wet clay floor. There was no ceiling. The sun overhead felt like a heating lamp.

"Getting a little thick, huh? Maybe you need

a bigger size," Zena said. She was already in her suit, smiling and sitting on a bench as she watched Zola struggle.

"Maybe you need to kiss my thick ass," Zola joked before giving the suit one final tug to get the zipper up. She exhaled to let her stomach loose and turned to look at herself in the mirror. "There we go," she said. "All ready."

"Got that right. Let's go show these Douglass boys how it's done," Zena said, standing to leave the locker room.

"Hey, Z. You remember what you said in the van?"

"What?" Zena stopped to look at Zola.

"About me—about me being able to do whatever I put my mind to."

"Yes."

"Did you mean it?" Zola asked.

"Why are you asking me this? Of course I do. Don't I always say that to you?"

"No. Not the way you said it just now."

"Come on," Zena said. "I'm always telling you that I believe in you."

"Yeah, but most times it's when you're trying to give me a pep talk—like to do something you want me to do. Not what I want to do," Zola pointed out. "When it's something I want to do, you say I can't do it. Or it's stupid. So, I always figured maybe you didn't mean it."

"I mean it always," Zena said, seriously feeling the weight of the moment. "You're a bright and driven woman."

"Thanks for coming with me," Zola said for probably the tenth time, but this one time it sounded different. And then she also repeated, "I couldn't do this without you."

Zola linked arms with Zena and began pulling her to the shore, where Alton and Adan were waiting with their surfboards.

"Hey, can I ask you something?" Zena started, hanging back a bit.

"What's up?"

"Did—" She paused before saying "Adan," as if maybe she shouldn't be saying his name. "Did Adan like say anything about me?"

"Like what?"

"I don't know. Anything?"

Zola looked off to recall. "He did say something about wanting to see you, like when we were back in Atlanta. He said he was trying to hook up with you, but you kept saying you were busy."

"He said, 'hook up'?" Zena repeated.

"No." Zola chuckled. "That doesn't even sound like Adan."

"I'm serious. What did he say? Like, exactly?" Zena pushed, while trying so hard to sound uninvolved, but her words and demeanor belied her intentions.

"Just that he wanted to see you, I think. To get up with you. You know?"

"Did he use the word *date*?" Zena stared at Zola as if her response could solve so many issues in the world.

"I don't know. I don't think so." Zola scrunched up her face. "Maybe. He could've." Zola stopped pondering and looked at Zena. "Wait—why are you so concerned? You turned him down. Are you having second thoughts?"

"Hell no," Zena answered, hardly giving Zola time to finish her question. "I just wanted to know."

Once the foursome was in the water and surfing along the beach break waves, it was quite clear to Zena that Abdul was wrong about the skill required to surf Padang Padang. The water was aggressive and filled with barrels ahead—water tubes created by rolling waves.

One of the instructors at the surf shop came out and gave Zola a short lesson, one Alton tried to avoid but then jumped in on because he clearly needed it after being knocked off his board a few times.

While Zena strategically kept her eye on Zola, noting that she was doing rather well on the waves and holding steady on her board, she and Adan charged the clean waves toward the middle of the beach break. They raced out, paddling quickly on their stomachs to get in the lineup with the other experienced surfers. Sometimes, the waves came between them and Zena couldn't see Adan, but when they subsided, there he was looking over at her smiling every time. She could see his brown arms moving around beneath the crystal clear water. He lifted his hand and pointed ahead toward the ocean. There was a barrel coming right toward them.

They hustled to their feet. Zena found her balance more quickly than she expected. Right foot over left. Lean right. Lean left. Ride the wave. Breathe. Balance the water in her body with the sea. She couldn't move against the water. If she did, she'd lose her balance. Come crashing down in the middle of the barrel, her body going one way, the board going the other.

Then Zena found herself in the middle of the barrel, an aquatic house in icy baby blue and emerald green all around her. She was standing on her board, measuring her weight, redistributing, trying to stay in the water house, but then she let go. She wanted to see it. To stop trying to be in it—and just see it.

She looked at the water spinning around her. Though it felt as if time had stopped, it was moving so fast, and this would only be her home for a few seconds. It was a magical moment for any surfer. Through the wave she could see the ocean, the shore. She looked to her left, and on the other side of a clear door of water there was Adan, standing upright beside her on his surfboard. His hand was reaching toward her. She tried to reach back toward him, but then the wave closed up and the sea spit Zena out in a yawn.

She fell to her board and wrapped her legs around the body, a rogue move one of Zena's surf instructors taught her to stop the board from spinning out beneath her.

When the water subsided, Zena sat up and found the surfers on the beach cheering her on. Zola and Alton were waving, and Zola screamed, "That's my big sister!"

"You still have it," Adan said.

Zena turned, and he was sitting on his board beside her in the water that had turned peaceful and soft.

"I guess you have it, too," Zena said. "I saw you in the barrel."

"I wasn't in the barrel."

"You reached for me!"

"Zena, I didn't make it. I clucked out when I saw that barrel. I wiped out and recovered just in time to see you perform."

"But I saw you." Zena clearly recalled Adan in the water bubble beside her.

More waves came, and Zena and Adan practiced cross steps and cutbacks. They laughed at each other as they fell off their boards. Looked after each other when the big waves came rolling through. They were talking without talking. Communicating. And it felt old. Comfortable. Familiar.

Zena and Adan watched and cheered as Zola and Alton conquered the scrappers, short waves closer to the shore.

Though she was far away, Zena could see a determination in Zola's stance on the board. Zola leaned forward, balancing her weight on her right knee as she spread her arms wide into a T to hold her balance on a dying wave beneath her board.

"Z! Look ahead!" Adan called, and hearing some sense of urgency in his voice, Zena snapped around to see a large wave, a big surf, headed their way. "Up!" Adan shouted. "Up!"

Zena popped to her feet in time to take off on the curl of the wave and ride the crest.

"Cowabunga!" she heard one of the shaggy long-haired Australian surfers nearby holler as he made his way through the wave.

Then she heard, "Swell!"—a surfer call meaning there would be waves of the same size and speed following right behind the one she was riding.

Zena steadied her toes on the edge of the board,

found her balance and held her breath as the water caught the board and flipped her over.

She wanted to curse but there was no time. She was underwater. Sand kicked up from the floor and bubbles burst all around her. She could see other surfers and their boards seeking reconnection in the blue.

Zena found her board and tugged at her ankle leash to bring it to her.

"You okay?" Adan asked, out of breath when she came up.

"Yeah, that was a tough one! Total wipeout!" Zena replied through her own bated breath as she sat up on her board.

"You ain't kidding." Adan nodded to the mess of struggling surfers gasping for air and trying to get back into the lineup to await the next wave.

Suddenly, and for no reason, because Zena hadn't surfed in months since her last vacation to Hawaii and seldom ever thought it, a word came to mind that shot fear through her body—the deep. This was the deepest part of a wave, the part near its peak where surfers were most often thrown wildly from their boards and accidents, sometimes tragic accidents, occurred in seconds.

There was an eerie quiet then. A damning calm.

"Zola?" Zena called, turning toward the direction of the swell that had passed them and gone

toward the shore, where Zola and Alton were practicing.

Zena spotted the surfing instructor and scanned
the water for Zola's brown face. She found Alton,
but he was staring out into the water blankly. She
searched backward and forward between the shore
and then the sea, and there was no Zola. "Zola?"

She could see Adan stand on his board and call
out to Alton. She couldn't make out what he was
saying because she was already paddling toward
the empty space where she'd last seen her sister.

She heard the lifeguard's whistle blow and saw
the instructor dive into the water.

A wild board popped up. But then no one followed.

"Zola!" Zena paddled faster, but she felt as if
she wasn't going anywhere and maybe she was
moving backward. She wanted to break from the
surfboard and swim, but removing the ankle strap
would take too long.

She saw Adan swim past, and every dark
thought she could ever imagine crept into her
brain, leaving a sinking suspicion that something
horrible was happening. "No! No!"

By the time Zena made it to shore, the lifeguards
were pulling Zola's limp body from the water.

Adan and Alton were racing behind them as
they made their way to the sand, where a crowd
had already gathered.

"My sister! My sister!" Zena screamed, and some surfer she didn't know helped her pull the ankle strap off before she was free from her surfboard and could run to Zola's side.

"Zola!" Zena pushed through the crowd of worried spectators and tried to get to Zola, but Adan stopped her.

"Wait!" he ordered Zena with his face as alarmed as hers. "Let them help her!"

There, on the sand, surrounded by lifeguards, lay a lifeless Zola. To Zena, Zola looked as if she was six years old, a child she was supposed to be looking after.

"Wake up, Zola! Wake up! Please!" Zena cried, trying to break away from Adan's hold as the crowd tightened.

One of the lifeguards straddled Zola and pressed heavily on her chest as another did mouth-to-mouth. Zena reached for Alton, who looked stunned, and grabbed his arm.

"You weren't watching her! Why weren't you watching her? You're so irresponsible!" she screamed at him.

"I was watching her! It just happened. She fell off her board when the big wave came. It wasn't my fault," he said. "Maybe if you would've told her to stay out of the water, this wouldn't have happened!"

Adan pulled them apart and said, "You two stop it! Zola is going to be fine."

As if Zola had heard Adan's command, water came sputtering out of her mouth. She gurgled and spat.

The crowd froze, and there was silence as they waited. This was a miracle in Bali.

Zola opened her eyes and looked around aimlessly. "Al-to," she made out. "Al…"

"I'm here!" Zena cried before she realized who Zola was calling for.

Alton pushed past Zena and went to Zola's side before she passed out again. "I'm here," he said.

The lifeguards rushed Zola to the infirmary at one of the hotels across the street from the beach. While everyone spoke English and seemed to be trying to help, Zena felt as if no one could understand her questions, and quickly this once-beautiful place had become a paradoxical hell of rushing and then waiting for word about Zola's condition.

Sitting outside of the one medical bed in the infirmary, where a petite nurse and off-duty vacationing doctor were meeting with Zola in private, Zena tried not to panic, but panic was all she felt.

"I don't understand why we can't just go to the hospital," Zena complained to Alton and Adan, who were standing before her and working to keep her in the seat so she wouldn't charge into the room to see Zola, as she'd done three times already.

"It's too far and it'll take too long for an ambulance to get here. Didn't you see that traffic out there?" Adan replied. "We went over this. And Zola's fine. She's already awake and talking to the doctor."

"But she could have internal bleeding, or something could be broken," Zena went on.

"*Zena*, she is fine!" Alton said.

"Well, you'd better hope she is, because if she's not—" Zena paused.

"What? What's that supposed to mean?" Alton asked.

"You know exactly what it means. What kind of husband are you going to be? You were supposed to be looking after her."

"She's not a child. I don't need to look after her. She's a grown woman," Alton argued. "And I was the one who told her not to get in the water. Or did you forget that?"

The nurse opened the door. Zena, Alton and Adan bum-rushed her, trying to get in to see Zola, but she announced that Zola was only ready to see one person and she'd requested Alton.

"But I'm blood. I'm next of kin here," Zena said, using her official courtroom tone with the nurse, who looked bored with Zena's comments and questions she'd endured since they'd rushed into the infirmary.

The nurse didn't respond. She signaled for Alton to follow her after letting the doctor out of the room.

"Ridiculous and unprofessional!" Zena complained, pivoting from the closed doors with her arms folded over her chest to demonstrate her discontent. "We should really just go to the hospital. Who knows if these people are even qualified to take care of Zola?"

"Zena, again, the hospital is too far, and the doctor said she's—" Adan was tired of comforting Zena's demands now, too. He stopped his repetitious response. "Look, why don't you do something? Like call your mother? Did you tell her what happened?"

"Call her for what? To tell her Zola fell off a surfboard and almost died?"

"She didn't almost die. She just slipped and got pulled in by the undercurrent. Scary, but not uncommon."

"You don't understand. If something happens to Zola, I'm the one who's responsible!" Zena cried, now hysterical. "I'm the one who's supposed to be watching her! I'm always the one watching!" Zena began to cry fresh, new tears that let on that this was about more than the sister sitting up doing just fine in the other room.

Adan pulled Zena into his arms and pressed her head to his chest. "It's all going to be fine," he said tenderly. "Don't worry. I'm here for you, baby."

Zena snapped back and pushed Adan away.

"Baby? I'm not your baby!" she hollered. "And you know what? Really, this is all on you! You!"

"Me?"

"Yes! You were the one who made this whole thing happen! We shouldn't even be here! Zola should be home in Atlanta studying for the Bar!"

"I thought you moved on from that, Zena."

"Moved on? From what? You clearly haven't moved on," Zena said. "And that's what this is all about."

"You don't know what you're talking about," Adan answered, walking away from Zena then, but she was right on his heels.

"How about I do. I know you're just doing this whole wedding thing because you're jealous!" Zena said.

"Jealous? Jealous of what?"

"Of me! And of Zola. That I was the one who made it, and now she was about to do the same. She was about to do what you couldn't do for Alton!"

"That's crazy. Look I'm excited about anything Zola does. She's like my little sister. She's like family."

"But she's *not* your family. We're not a couple. You blew that!"

"I know I did, and I'm so sorry. Don't you think that's haunted me every day since we broke up?"

The door cracked open again, and all words stopped as Adan and Zena rushed over for news.

"Is she okay?" Adan asked as Alton walked out.

"She's fine," Alton confirmed. He looked at Zena. "She wants to see you now."

Zena wiped her tears and walked into the room as if she expected to see Zola hooked up on life support and completely covered in a full-body cast.

Reality was the opposite.

The sun was shining through the window of what looked like a dorm room, and Zola was sitting up smiling as if she was just waking up and had never set foot on the beach.

"You have to be kidding me!" Zola joked, getting an eyeful of her sister's countenance. "You're crying? I thought I heard you out there hollering."

She reached for Zena and hugged her before moving over so Zena could sit on the bed.

"How are you feeling?" Zena asked.

"I'm fine. I just lost my step, and then I felt the water pulling me back. I panicked," Zola explained. "I probably shouldn't have been in that water anyway."

"You were fine. I saw you on the board. I was watching you. I really was," Zena pleaded.

"You didn't need to watch me, Z. What happened wasn't anyone's fault. It was a freak accident."

"No, it wasn't a freak accident. We shouldn't be here. Look, I've been trying to accept this wedding and support you, but I shouldn't have let you come here," Zena said. "And I don't know why Adan is supporting this, but it's a mistake. It's clearly a mistake. You shouldn't be getting married. And maybe this is just a sign."

Zola pursed her lips, and then her own tears began to fall.

"What? What's wrong?" Zena asked. "Is it something I said? Because I'm just telling the truth. I'm not trying to hurt you. It's for your own good—"

"No," Zola cut in. "It's not you. It's me. It's about what I haven't told you." She looked off at the sunlight coming through the window and exhaled. "There's a reason Alton was nervous about me getting on the surfboard. It was ridiculous that he thought it would have any impact, but I know why he was scared. He was just looking out for me."

"What are you talking about? Why was he scared?"

Zola looked at Zena.

"I had a miscarriage," Zola said, the sad words slipping out of her mouth just one per second.

"What? When?" Zena placed her hand on Zola's knee.

"A few days before graduation. I was just so stressed and worried about everything and I woke up one morning and..." She paused and looked into Zena's eyes. "I lost my baby."

"Did you know you were pregnant?"

"I suspected. But I didn't even have any time to take the test. I think I was scared to know. I was terrified to know, because it meant everything was about to change. Everything I wanted was gone," Zola said.

"That's not true. And why didn't you tell me? Why didn't you call me or something?" Zena asked.

"The last thing you said to me before you left DC my first year of law school was that I shouldn't get pregnant," Zola said. "And there I was—pregnant."

"You should've told me, Zola. I would've been there for you."

"The funny thing is when I was at the hospital and I realized there was no way Alton could get to me, the only other person I wanted to call was you, but I just couldn't. It would be like I was letting myself down by just saying it to you. So, I called the next best person."

"Mommy?"

"No, Z. I called Adan."

"What?"

"He actually left his job in New York and flew to DC. Six hours after I called, he was by my side."

Zena jumped up from the bed and began pacing.

"You should've called *me*," she protested.

"You're not listening."

"I *am* listening. And I'm telling you that you should've called *me* and not Adan!" Zena turned to Zola.

"No, *you're* not listening. I'm trying to tell you something."

"Tell me what?"

"Adan has always been there for me. He visited me in DC more than you. More than anyone else— other than Alton," Zola revealed. "And when it was clear I needed help, like more help just to get through graduation, he paid for me to go to therapy. He was at my graduation, too. He sat alone, though…because he knew you'd be upset if you knew he was there. But he said he couldn't stay away. He knew I needed him there."

Zola got off the bed and went to stand before Zena.

"That's what this wedding is about. Why Adan is supporting it. It has nothing to do with Alton. It's about me. About me getting better," Zola said.

"So you've been communicating with him all this time and not telling me?" Zena asked.

"We all have. Me. Mommy. Malak. We just

don't tell you because we know how you'll get. We know how you get about him," Zola said. "I mean, you didn't even go to Mrs. Pam's funeral because he'd be there. After all she did for us, you—"

"I couldn't!" Zena shouted, cutting Zola off.

"I know. And I understand. Going through this, I completely understand how hard it can be to move on sometimes," Zola said. "And maybe it's time for you to admit to yourself that you haven't."

"I have."

"Just give him a chance."

"I've moved on!"

"He deserves a chance."

"For what?"

"You guys were just kids then. He was making the best decision he could. He thought he was doing the right thing," Zola said. "And you know that."

"What he thought doesn't matter. What he did does."

"He still loves you, Z," Zola confessed.

"You don't know what you're talking about."

Zola smirked at Zena's uneasiness. "You asked if he mentioned wanting to take you on a date? I don't remember that. But I do remember what he told me about you—about how he feels about you."

"What?" Zena asked, and then she turned from her sister. "Never mind, I don't want to know."

"He said he loves you. He still loves you, and he'd do anything to be back with you. I hope you give him that chance."

Chapter 7

Zola stayed in Alton's bed that night.

In the minivan on the way back to Mahatma House, Zena had watched Zola and Alton comforting each other, Zola resting her head on Alton's shoulder, him kissing her forehead, and it was as if she was spying something new in them and really seeing their love for one another for the first time—their adult love for one another for the first time. They were no longer teens falling asleep on the phone together. They were grown folks whose love had been tested, been through some things, and there they were, still holding on to each other.

Dinner was endured in silence. No speeches.

No tactics. They ate and let the ocean breeze play its melody of life moving on.

Zena could hardly look at Adan across the dinner table.

And he hardly looked at her.

The news she had, the news he knew she'd been given at the infirmary, was about to change everything. It had to. How could it not?

After dinner, Zena stood in the mirror of her black cocoon remembering the laughs she'd had with Adan before Zola's accident. How something as simple as surfing in the Indian Ocean had become a kind of temporary peacekeeping activity between the two in a time of war. Adan hadn't seemed like an enemy then. He didn't seem all-powerful. Or all evil. He didn't want to hurt her. He was just a man with brown skin and a smile she knew well.

Zena remembered his reaching for her in the barrel. Her reaching back. Him saying he hadn't been there wrapped in water with her, and then the vision of him in the barrel being clearer than it was when it happened. Was he telling the truth about wiping out? Why would he lie? And if he wasn't there, what had she seen? Was she seeing what she wanted to see?

"I needed you! I needed you to be there for me!" Zena was standing face-to-face with Adan at the door of his villa at Mahatma House. When she felt these words boiling in her gut in the mirror, she'd run out of her room and across the property in her panties and a tank top to say this to him—to his face. "I needed you more than anything. More than some stupid degree and some stupid dream of being a lawyer. I needed you to stay with me."

"Zena, I know. And I'm sorry. I'm so sorry that I—"

"No! Wait! I'm not here for that. I'm not here for an apology. I'm here to tell you that I know now. I know that as much as I needed you, Adan, you couldn't be there for me," Zena said. "It wasn't your job to be there for me." Zena paused as she began to cry, feeling so much hurt she'd tried to keep hidden in her hate of Adan. "You're not my father. You can't make up for his failures. You had your own life to live."

"No. I didn't."

"What?"

"Look, why don't you come in and we can talk about this." Adan glanced down at Zena's nude legs. "I can give you some pants to put on."

"Oh, my God!" Zena was embarrassed by her lack of clothes and remembered her rush to Adan. She hadn't felt a thing—not one chill or breeze against her legs in the heat of the night. "What am I doing? Why am I here?" She tried to turn to leave, but Adan stopped her.

"No. Don't go. I understand." Adan pointed

down at his jeans and the flip-flops on his feet. "I was actually on my way to you. To talk to you." He grinned at her. "But I took some time to put on the proper attire."

Adan pulled Zena inside and gave her a pair of his jogging shorts.

They agreed to walk to the shore behind the villa, where they could talk.

There was a cool breeze there from the water, but it still did little to contend with the heat that was emanating from the sand that had been baking all day.

"I know I sounded like a complete jerk. I couldn't think of anything else to say, though," Adan said, recalling his explanation to Zena about why he was supporting Alton and Zola's wedding outside Madame Lucille's Lace weeks before.

Now that Zena understood his predicament with Zola, his flimsy and seemingly selfish excuse sounded plausible.

"I wanted to tell you to mind your business, but I know you too well for that," Adan said after he and Zena had a good laugh at her digging into him that day.

"I wasn't that bad," Zena said. "I was just looking out for my little sister." She looked at Adan and said with clear sincerity, "And I'm glad you looked out for her when she needed you. I can't imagine what she went through."

"I was thankful I could be there. You know? I meant what I said earlier—she's like my sister. I don't want to ever see her in pain. And she did take the miscarriage pretty hard. The only thing that seemed to give her hope was the idea of someday marrying Alton and actually having a baby."

"So, that's how you all came up with the wedding?"

Adan answered, "Felt like a step in the right direction. We all know where those two are headed. I don't think I've ever seen two people who love one another more than them."

There was an awkward pause and step as the word *love* settled between Adan and Zena. It was clear there was something more they needed to discuss that they just couldn't. This was where they were comfortable—talking about other people and their love, but not what they'd had. Maybe that would be too much or too forward. Maybe it would break something in the new connection they might be forging. Both wondered this in step and in silence, but then Adan just stopped walking and looked up at the moon with a certain fire that gave Zena hope he might break that silence. Remembering everything Zola had told her at the infirmary, she was ready to hear something then. She was ready to tell her truth. She wasn't over Adan. She hadn't ever gotten over him or how it ended. She turned to look at the moon, too.

"You remember that day?" Adan asked in a question with little detail, but still Zena knew his point of reference.

"The corner of Sassafras Street and Blue Stone Road," Zena announced.

"Someone else had to see it," Adan said, still transfixed on the glowy moon in Bali. "Never made sense to me that we were the only ones. I asked everyone, though. No one knew what I was talking about."

"A celestial event." Zena had been standing behind Adan in the sand, but she stepped beside him when she said this.

"An eclipse for two," Adan repeated their science teacher Mr. Palabas's explanation of their spectacular view of the sky's magic.

Zena didn't know what to say to that. She thought she could simply nod in agreement, but then that felt wrong, so she just stood there staring at the moon with Adan.

After a while, he said, "Zena, I've missed you. I've missed you so much that sometimes I felt like it was going to kill me. That's how bad it ached."

Zena heard Adan's breathing quicken as if he'd just dropped something heavy from his arms.

"I had to say that," he said, and then he took another deep breath. "I had to say it." He turned to Zena and looked at her profile.

"Don't!" Zena ordered when she felt he was

about to speak again. Tears were already streaming down to her chin. She didn't know what she was afraid of hearing, what she didn't want to hear. But with those words from Adan, she felt in her heart that same aching he was describing. She knew it well, too. The feeling of being apart. The feeling of being without him had been too much on too many days. And right then, recalling it all was like pouring salt on those injuries.

"I have to," Adan said. "I have to say it all. And I know you don't want me to respond to what you said earlier, but I have to. I have to tell you that I should've been there for you. Your heart was my responsibility. I knew you needed me. And I was a fool for leaving you."

"But we were just kids. You were right. We needed to go out into the world. And follow our dreams," Zena said with Adan's old words in her mouth.

"No. We were kids who were lucky enough to have found our dreams in each other. I know that now. I've spent my whole adult life paying for not seeing that. That's why I couldn't get married. I called it off because I realized I was just making up for not having you. I was just pretending that everything was great, but it never would be. Not if you weren't there."

Adan went to stand between Zena and her locked view on the moon.

She closed her eyes to avoid his presence.

"Look at me," he said softly.

Tears continued to escape from her closed eyes.

"No," Zena uttered.

"Look at me!" Adan began to wipe Zena's tears and slid his hand beneath her chin. "Please, just see me."

He lifted her head, and Zena slowly opened her eyes.

"I know I'm supposed to be cool. I know I'm supposed to have a more elaborate plan to win you back and pay off your pain, but I don't have that. All I have is the truth," Adan said. "Yes, I supported this wedding because I wanted to help Zola and Alton. But I knew there was no way Zola would do this without you. And I wanted to see you." Adan moved his hand to caress Zena's cheek. "And I wanted to see you so I could say these things to you."

"Why?" Zena asked.

"Because I want to be with you."

"Be with me? But we haven't been together in nine years. It's been so long. Too long."

"Stop it, Z. Stop it with that wall! Just stop," Adan said, and then he started crying, too. "I'm Adan! You can let it down. I'm here. I'm here. I'm here. And I love you. I love you so much."

Did Adan pull Zena to him for that kiss that followed these words? Or was Zena the one who

pulled Adan to her lips? Neither would ever know
or remember. But it happened. It was as if the
space between them in the sand evaporated and
their toes touched and then their lips connected
and then there was a kiss.

Zena closed her eyes and felt Adan's arms wrap-
ping around her, holding her up and steadying her
against his body. She didn't want to let go of his
lips. She didn't want to be released from his hold.
But still, she wondered, *What is this? What is happening?*

She opened her eyes to see him, to confirm that
this was him and look at Adan as he kissed her
so passionately.

And he was there. Adan was before her with
his eyes closed and joy written all over his face.

Twinkling or sparkling behind his right ear
caught Zena's eye. She refocused and saw something that looked like fireworks, but then she knew
it couldn't be, so she broke the lip-lock from Adan
and ordered him to turn around.

"Look! Look!" she screamed, pointing at the
shining clear black night.

As soon as Adan turned, in one second there
was a flicker and pop, and two shooting stars raced
across the sky.

"Did you see that? Did you see that?" Zena
rushed out, still in shock at what she'd just seen.

"Yes! I did! I did! I think it was a shooting

star—two shooting stars!" Adan said with his voice half-confused or in awe.

"Oh, my God! I can't believe we just saw that!" Zena was ecstatic then and jumping in the sand. She turned to Adan and said with significant cadence, "We just saw that. We just saw that together. Right as we kissed."

Adan began to lower his head to kiss Zena again, but then he had a thought: "Wait!" he said, stopping himself right before Zena's anticipating lips. "I wonder if anyone else saw it!"

"Who cares? It was just for us," Zena said before pulling Adan's face down to hers and kissing him again.

Inside Adan's room, there were no strangers, no nervous energy, no pretense or discussion about what should or could happen.

With the sound of waves rolling in the distance and the moon peeking into the slightly slanted shutters, in the darkness of the villa, Adan slid off Zena's clothes and knelt down to study her body as if it was something he'd cherished but lost and then found again. He closed his eyes as he kissed her stomach and caressed the outsides of her thighs. Into her navel he spoke of love and never letting go again. Still on his knees, he wrapped his arms around her waist and rested his head over the top of her vagina. He held her and waited as if he was meditating or praying. He held Zena there in that position for so long she didn't want to move him. To say a thing. To ask a thing.

Soon, Zena began to cry again. She palmed the top of his head and said, "I forgive you and I missed you. And… I love you, too."

Chapter 8

Zola was sitting at the breakfast table, holding Alton's hand so tightly neither could eat their food. She looked as if nothing happened the day before and was so perky and cheerful no one wanted to bring it up. While it was another lazy, hot morning in Bali, it was her wedding day and all knew she should enjoy the bliss moments like this could bring without interruption.

Over postbreakfast green tea, as the foursome debated the event of the double shooting star, Zena watched Zola and thought of how different she seemed than any other bride on their wedding day, at least the ones Zena had seen. Most were rushing and running, rummaging and ruling over everything. Their grooms were hidden away; their world was an oiled machine of pomp and circumstance that had to go just as planned. This circus grew and evolved until it ended with the bride looking exhausted and tuned out, ready to escape to the refuge of a honeymoon hours away. But here was Zola sitting at the breakfast table in a thin turquoise sundress they'd purchased in the market downtown. Her hair was up in her topknot and she had two ridiculously large hibiscuses tucked behind each ear. She looked like some Bohemian garden nymph, completely relaxed and just happy. She was already on her honeymoon and neither bothered nor vexed about what lay ahead.

"Bruh, there's no such thing as a double shooting star!" Alton teased Adan. "It just doesn't make sense. The spontaneity behind the single scientific event of one star shooting across the sky—and while two people are watching—is just too rare for two to occur at once—and, again, while two people are watching."

"What, are you an astronomer now? You hardly graduated from Clark Atlanta, and now you sound like freaking Neil deGrasse Tyson," Adan said, and everyone laughed.

"I watch documentaries on Netflix. I know many things!" Alton followed up, and then the laughter grew at his response.

"Seriously, though, there were two shooting stars. I saw it, too," Zena confirmed. "It was so fast. But I saw it. I know I saw it."

By then, Zena and Adan had questioned most everyone at Mahatma House, including the security guard and the beautiful long-haired girl who showed up each morning to do the flower offering at the villa's traditional altar. They wanted to know if anyone had seen the shooting stars. No one had seen a thing. And two people, the chef and the woman who cleaned Adan's room, confirmed that they'd indeed been looking at the sky at that exact hour and hadn't witnessed anything out of the norm.

"Maybe you did—maybe you didn't," Zola said. "The real question is, why were both of you looking up at the sky at the same time after midnight? That's what I want to know." Zola grinned and looked from Adan to Zena. They were sitting beside one another and looking very cozy. They weren't touching, but their bodies were still leaning into each other with enough normalcy to reveal the tale from the night before.

Suddenly, they moved apart after hearing Zola's question. Both felt the need to clear their throats. They looked like teenagers who'd been caught kissing.

"What!" Zola's grin grew to a full smile.

"Did something happen?" Alton asked, intrigued by their behavior, too.

"We just talked," Adan answered with forced calm in his voice. He patted Zena on her back. "Just had a friendly chat on the beach."

Zola looked unconvinced and kept her big smile. "Friendly, huh? I bet it was. I bet it also describes why, when I came to Zena's room this morning to drop off her maid of honor dress, she wasn't there."

"Actually," Zena followed quickly, "I'd gone for an early-morning jog."

Zola came back with, "*Actually*, I tripped over your sneakers when I walked into the room. Soooo..."

Adan and Zena held in their laughter at being caught as Alton and Zola traded stares.

Zena worked hard to shift the conversation from the topic of her whereabouts the night before by asking Zola and Alton about their wedding plans. They revealed that they'd decided to take a short walk through the village to the hut of a local Balian Tenung, a diviner, who would bless them before their ceremony.

After breakfast, Zola followed Zena back to her villa to try on their dresses and have Zena braid her hair. The dresses had arrived that morning, and while Zola had already tried on her dress, Zena hadn't even seen her dress.

As soon as Zola closed the sliding door of the villa and turned around to Zena, she begged, "Tell me everything that happened! I want to know it all! Everything!"

"Nothing happened. It was just a walk," Zena said, knowing Zola was referring to the events with Adan.

"You know I'm not stupid, right? I may have nearly killed myself in the ocean yesterday, but I didn't incur any brain damage. I'm operating with all my cards in the deck!"

Zena plopped down on the bed and sighed helplessly, the way a woman does when she's resolved that she's in love.

"Everything happened," she said. *"Everything."*

"Oh, girl, this sounds too good!" Zola sat down beside Zena and leaned over for gossip. "I'll get to that second everything later, but give me the first everything now."

"You're a mess. Look, he just told me he loves me and that he wants to be with me."

"I know all that, Zena. That's not news. I'm asking for the goods. What did you say?"

"I…I," Zena stuttered to try to find her words to reveal what she'd said to Adan, but Zola stopped her.

"Tell me the truth. Even if you didn't tell him

the truth. Tell me the truth. Tell me what you wanted to say," the younger sister ordered wisely.

Zena looked at Zola as if she was the big sister.

"I said it. I admitted it." She paused and remembered standing before Adan. "I admitted that I was in love with him. And that I've missed him. And I've been so sad without him. All these years."

Zola's back stiffened, and she pulled Zena's head to her chest. She kissed her forehead and smiled. Both knew the weight of Zena's admission to Adan. This was an act of fearlessness from a brave woman, who mistakenly thought the most selfless thing she could do was keep Adan away, but the real fear to face was letting him back in. This was peeking under the bed to find ghosts.

As she set up to braid Zola's hair, Zena went on with her recall about the shooting stars, Adan's kiss and him picking her up to carry her all the way to his villa. Zola listened to all of this. "Ya'll are back in love," Zola proclaimed. "Finally back in love."

"Well, I don't know all of that. I don't know where this is going from here. If it's going anywhere. I'm just happy we got it off our chests. It was cathartic."

Zola laughed. "Right. You can say that to everyone else," she said. "You can believe it if you want. Just know that's not what Adan's thinking."

"What's he thinking?"

"He's already purchased a condo downtown—

three blocks from you. And he's moving to Atlanta as soon as we get back."

"But that couldn't have anything to do with me. He didn't know how I'd react to him. If anything would happen between us," Zena said.

"I don't think he cared. I think he intended to keep trying. See, Adan thinks I'm slow. I know what this wedding thing was about. He was looking out for me, but he was also trying to win you back."

When Zola got up to look at her braids in the mirror, Zena revealed that Adan admitted that the night before but added that she was sure Zola was his chief concern.

"Well, I guess we'd better get this show on the road, then," Zola said. She left the mirror and reached for the garment bag containing Zena's maid of honor dress hanging on a hook beside the bed. "I tried to get in here earlier so you could try this thing on. I hope it fits. We won't have time for changes."

"I'm sure it'll be fine. I think I've actually lost weight since Madame Lucille took my measurements at the shop," Zena joked.

"Yeah. Right! You wish!" Zola winked and unzipped the bag, revealing a sleek bumblebee-yellow, single-shoulder satin robe with a thin cream waist bodice. The stylish dress was a mix of vintage chic and sophistication that immediately stole a smile from Zena.

Zena was up on her feet walking to the dress with her hands over her mouth to exemplify her awe and excitement. "This is for me? For me?"

Zola pulled the bag from the hook and let it fall to the floor, fully displaying her dress selection for her sister. "Yes."

Zena didn't know if she should hug Zola or go for the dress, so she did both. She took the dress from the wall and pulled Zola into an embrace. "I love it. I really love it."

"I helped Madame Lucille design it. I wanted something really special for you."

"But it's too much. No? Like, it looks like something that could be for a bride." Zena let Zola go and inspected the dress by holding the hanger out. "It's just that beautiful."

Zola was looking at Zena look at the dress. With pride, she said, "A beautiful dress for my beautiful sister."

"Oh, thank you, Zollie."

"Seriously. I really wanted to design something amazing for you. Something to show how special you are to me," Zola explained. "This day isn't just about me and Alton. It's about you, too. About everything you've done for me—how you've been there for me. For us."

"Of course, I'm there for you. You're my baby sister," Zena said.

"It's more than that. You know it. You've been

more than a sister. You've been a mother. A father. You've been there for me when I had no one.
And you've believed in me," Zola continued. "Last
night, after the accident on the beach, that's all I
kept thinking about—you believe in me. Sometimes
more than I've believed in myself. You see things in
me that no one else can see. And I know for sure in
my life that it has made all the difference."

The dress fell over Zena's skin as if she'd grown
into it, as if it was a part of her.

Zola went to the bathroom to finish looking
over her appearance. There was a soft knock at
the door. Zena thought it was the housekeeper, so
she quickly opened it up only to find Adan standing there in a tan linen suit. Somehow, Zena felt
Adan shouldn't be seeing her dress, so she covered her chest as if she was a bride and he was
getting a peek.

"I'm sorry," Adan said, covering his eyes.

"Wait! Wait!" Zena laughed, realizing her error.
"I'm tripping. I'm not the bride. You can clearly
look at my dress." She laughed.

"Really?" Adan asked, still covering his eyes.
"Are you sure?"

"Yes, silly." Zena smiled at Adan's playing. He
looked handsome in his suit. Not too pretentious
or formal. He was dapper but relaxed.

He lowered his hand and peeked at Zena. "I
don't know. I don't want to get in trouble. You

women and your wedding-day rules about people seeing your dress."

"Well, it's not my wedding day so you can see my dress."

"Well, I was just coming over here before things get started to make sure you're fine."

"I'm fine," Zena said. "Why wouldn't I be? Shouldn't I be?" She looked at Adan curiously, as if maybe he was seeing their evening exchange differently than she had. She hoped he hadn't.

"I'm just wondering if you feel like I feel." Adan grinned in a way that made him look fifteen years old again. Right then, Zena felt as if they were back in Georgia, back on their street, blushing at each other. "Look, I'm just excited." Adan looked at Zena. "That's the best way I can put it. I'm excited. I'm happy it happened. And, I guess, I came to say I hope you're happy, too."

Zena leaned into the door frame before Adan. "I am," she admitted.

"Great." Adan's smile grew as he stepped back from the door to return to Alton. "I'm happy to hear that, because this is all I've wanted for a long time."

The next knock at the door was Kadek, the villa manager. He arrived ready to escort the sisters to the front gate. Adan and Alton were waiting there to begin the short walk to the beach hut where the Balian Tenung would bless Alton and Zola before the wedding ceremony. He was carrying a huge parasol made of iridescent silks and gold piping. Curly sheer fabric dangled from each corner.

"You ready?" Zena asked, looking at Zola standing in front of the mirror, nervously adjusting the crown of wild shore flowers she'd collected to decorate the goddess braids Zena put in her hair. The rose-gold lace sheath Lisa had picked out for Zola at Lucille's Lace was simple yet ethereal.

"Guess I have to be," Zola said. "Let's do this."

Zola began to walk to the door, but Zena suddenly felt she needed to add some words, some weight to the moment before Zola went to say her vows.

"I didn't come here with the best of intentions," she said.

"What?"

"I thought I was coming here to stop you from marrying Alton. I thought I could use my relationship with you as leverage to keep you from saying, 'I do.' But now, with everything that's happened, I know I was wrong. I know I was just holding you back from getting what you really want. And I know it's just my job to make sure you get that."

Zola responded, "You were just trying to have my back. I can't be mad at you for that. I'm only happy you're in my corner right now."

The sisters hugged, and Zena gave Zola a big kiss on the cheek.

"I wish Mommy could see you in this dress," Zena said. "I really wish she could've been here."

"Me, too."

Zola pulled Zena out the door, and the two floated under the colorful celebratory parasol toward the front gate.

When Zola spotted Alton and Adan standing there, she ran ahead of Zena and Kadek, kicking up her dress so all could see her gold gladiator sandals. She ran so fast it was as if she hadn't seen Alton in days or weeks, months. Or maybe it was as if she'd never seen him before and had only known him in dreams and this was their first time laying eyes on one another.

And he ran toward her, also. Standing beside Adan in his matching tan linen suit with a blooming bright yellow allamanda in his lapel that matched Zena's dress, Alton dropped his guitar and ran to meet Zola halfway on the path to the gate. He picked her up and held her in the air as if she was light as a flower petal.

Pretending to fly, Zola spread her arms out and hollered, "I love you, Alton Douglass!"

"Come on now. You two aren't even married yet. Calm down with the drama!" Adan joked from behind Alton and Zola. He walked over to Zena and kissed her on the forehead before putting one arm around her shoulder.

"Thank you!" Zena jumped in. "Let's save all the mushy stuff until after the legal stuff."

Alton and Zola guffawed at the elder siblings' comments and got in line to walk to the beach. Alton picked up his guitar and set out in the back of the crowd, playing a simple and sweet melody he'd played on many nights to lull Zola to sleep.

Kadek led the party, carrying the parasol in the front as they paraded through the small, rude and rocky streets of the country town that was busy with afternoon business. Lean-to shop owners and smiling locals came out to see the party pass. Some offered their blessings and others came out to tie ornate ribbons to Zena's and Zola's waists, a symbolic blessing of good luck and prosperity. Small children wanted to shake Zola's hand. One woman stepped up for a picture with the bridal party. This part of the journey appeared foreign from any wedding celebration they'd ever seen, but it also felt natural and intimate. As if it was the way that love ought to be celebrated, in the community, without excessive flair, with much love beneath the sun.

When they entered the portion of the beach that led to the Balian Tenung's hut, Kadek lowered the parasol and pointed to a small temple that had been meticulously decorated with flowers and sitting statues by the Tenung's followers and visitors throughout the years. It looked like a whimsical beach cabin or fairy-tale hideout. Two burning torches demarked the entrance. A little closer to the shore, a wooden altar and gazebo was overrun with fresh-picked fragrant plumeria. The Catatan Sipil, civil registrar, Adan hired to officiate over Alton and Zola's vows stood awaiting the occasion of the nuptials beneath the gazebo.

"Before marriage, you see Nyoman inside. He ready for you," Kadek said, pointing to the hut. "You go together. He bless you. Good for marriage."

Inside the hut, the foursome found a short, plump man with a bald head and few teeth sitting in the lotus position on a torn wool mat. Draped in white muslin, he smiled politely, said a few words to welcome them and gestured for them to sit before him.

For seconds or minutes, he glanced at their eyes, moving from one to the next, peeking wisely and knowingly at something that made each of them feel awkward but lucky to be in Nyoman's presence. He didn't look like a wise man, though, not like the stereotypical truth teller most Western visitors expected to see sitting in the hut. Nyoman appeared cheerful yet studied. He might be a schoolteacher or a chef—judging from his stomach—if he wasn't sitting in that hut.

"You love—you all love each other," he said finally. "You together. Always stay together. Always."

He signaled for Adan and Zena to join hands.

"Oh, no, we're not the ones getting married," Zena said as softly as she could, so as not to disturb the quiet in the space. "They are." She pointed to Zola and Alton sitting beside her.

Nyoman looked down at his lap and waited.

"You here for marry," he said as the sounds and breeze of the rolling tide outside crashed into the doorway. He looked up at Adan and added, "You here for love her. You here for marry her." He pointed to Zena.

The words were a secret spoken aloud. There was an uncomfortable chuckle from the foursome, with Zena leading. But Nyoman did not budge. He did not smile.

"Your heart is without cover," he said then to Zena. "He cover your heart. He give heart to you safe." He reached over and patted the ground before Zena's and Adan's locked hands. "You together. You love."

"But—" Zena tried, but her desired interrogation was met with a firm eye from Nyoman. There would be no more questions.

He lifted his hand and turned to Alton with his guitar and Zola with her wildflowers in her hair. He smiled at them as if they were children frolicking in a meadow.

"Love of flower in garden," he said to them.

"Flower no open. Flower closed. No pluck. No time. Soon time. Soon time pluck flower."

Zena looked over at Zola to see her stare at Nyoman, drinking in his words.

Alton wrapped his arm over Zola's shoulders and kissed her cheek, but she never once looked away from Nyoman.

"Well, we're about to pluck it right now, right outside," Adan joked in an attempt to break the stare between Nyoman and Zola.

Nyoman smiled and then reached into one of the copper bowls of water and uncooked rice on the floor between them. He uttered foreign words and placed the water and rice on each person's forehead with his thumb.

Kadek appeared in the doorway to escort them to the gazebo for the nuptials.

As the caravan rose to depart, Zena noticed Zola lingering in the back, still looking at Nyoman sitting there in the lotus position with a satisfied smile on his face.

She caught Zola's arm. "Are you all right?" Zena asked.

"I'm fine." Zola looked at Zena, and in Zola's eyes, Zena found some state of serenity, of enlightenment.

The sisters clasped hands and sojourned up the twisting strip of sand heading toward the plumeria-draped gazebo, where the civil registrar presiding over the ceremony was standing beside Adan and Alton, who was strumming his song on the guitar to entice his bride down the aisle to him.

While the melody was the same, he'd changed the words for that special day:

> Kiss me and I know your heart is pure.
> Love me and I swear I'll give you more.
> You are my love, my breath to carry me away.
>   You are my life—my days will be the same.

Some of the villagers who'd followed the procession to the beach had formed a thin circle before the gazebo. They waved and threw fresh-picked flowers at Zola and Zena as they walked by.

As Zena escorted Zola, she looked ahead at Adan standing beside his little brother. He was smiling, but unlike everyone else, his eyes weren't on the bride; he was watching Zena. He was staring at her. His gaze was so focused, in fact, that Zena looked away. She felt that if she'd kept her eyes on him, she might walk straight to him, forget where she was and what she was supposed to be doing, and stand by his side.

When the women reached the men, Zena kissed Zola on the cheek and stepped to the side.

The registrar, a little man with seesaw shoulders, began to read through his legal proceedings, nodding to Zola and Alton to be sure both understood his shaky English.

He paused and announced that the couple wanted to state their own vows.

Alton spoke first: "Zola, I don't remember any part of my life without you. Or else, maybe, all the parts before you, were me trying to get to you. Trying to make you see me. And when you did, when you finally saw me, it was like my life began again. And I never want it to end. Zola, I vow to be your partner. I vow to be by your side. I vow to be in your corner. You don't have to look for me. You don't have to call my name. I vow to just be there."

Zola wiped tears from Alton's cheeks and then stood still so he could wipe hers.

The registrar turned to her.

The sea breeze took on an expectant howl as new seconds ticked past. There was waiting for something to happen, and then there was this—awkward lagging where there should have been words—words from Zola.

There was near-inaudible chatter from the onlookers. Zena smiled at them and nudged Zola in the back.

The registrar lacked any Westernized notion of sympathy for those in contemplation at such times, so he kept a stare on Zola's eyes, which were solemn and maybe mournful by then.

"Zola!" Zena nudged Zola again and called her name rather unceremoniously.

"Alton, I love you but—" Zola started, but then her voice cracked and she looked down at her feet.

Not knowing what was happening or what to do, Zena grabbed her elbow as if she was afraid Zola was about to topple over.

"It's okay," Alton said softly. "It's really okay, Z. We don't have to. It's okay."

"What? What's okay?" Zena said, pulling Zola's arm then. She looked past Alton at Adan for help, but he appeared just as confused as she felt.

"I can't," Zola whispered to her gold gladiator sandals, but her voice was clear and distinct enough for all around to hear the two condemning words one should never say at an altar.

"I know, baby. It's fine," Alton said, his voice supportive and encouraging.

Zola found some strength and looked up at Alton with more tears and different tears streaming down. Firmly, she said, "I can't do this."

The registrar had forgotten his provisional English and was speaking harsh words in his native Balinese.

"I understand," Alton said as Adan leaned over to him to say something in his ear.

"No wedding?" the registrar said to Zola.

Before Zola could answer, Zena said over her to the registrar, "Yes, wedding! Yes!"

In a rush, she grabbed Zola's hand and tugged her down the steps leading away from the gazebo to the beach.

With nowhere to go, she stopped maybe a quarter of a mile from Alton and Adan and with all eyes on her, she asked Zola what was going on.

"I can't do it. I don't want to get married right now," Zola said. "You heard Nyoman. It's not time."

"Who cares what that old man said? It's Alton. You love him," Zola argued.

"I do love him and I do want to marry him, but I don't think I want to do it now."

"But we're here. That's why we're all here, because you said you wanted to marry him *now*."

"I think I was doing it because I thought it was going to make me feel better about—" Zola looked off to the water; one of the wildflowers dropped from her crown and floated away in the breeze. "But it hasn't. And I don't think marrying Alton will make anything better. It'll just make everything different."

Zena reached out and touched her shoulder. "Did you tell him this?"

"We talked about it last night a little—well, a lot. He knows how I feel. But I said I'd still go through with it." Zola looked back at Zena. "I don't think I can. Not now."

"Zola, I hope nothing I said changed your mind.

I love Alton, and I know you two belong together," Zena said.

Zola replied, "No. It's not you—well, I guess it is, in a way.

"Oh, no! I'm sorry. I—"

"No. Listen. I'm not talking about you discouraging me. I'm talking about you encouraging me," Zola said. "Another thing Alton and I talked about last night is me taking the Bar Exam. I'm going to do it."

"What?" Zena pushed surprised.

"I was scared and I was worried and I know now that some of this wedding stuff was also about me putting that off. I can admit that. And I can also admit that you're right. It is time for me to take the test. You believing in me helped me believe in myself."

"So what are we going to do?" Zena spied the confused crowd. "You know I'll support you in whatever you want to do, but these people are expecting a wedding."

"You know...they can still see a wedding," Adan said, suddenly stepping into view. "They will see a wedding if you say yes to marrying me."

Adan reached for Zena's hand. With no hesitation, he got down on his left knee and asked her, "Zena Nefertiti Shaw, will you marry me?"

Zena felt something in her heart humble under

those words, something break away and wither. It was pain. It was gone.

"Yes," she said. "Yes!"

Seeing this, the crowd cheered. Adan stood and grabbed Zena's hand, racing back to the gazebo, with Zola close behind.

The crowd, which had now doubled in size, began to applaud their return.

"Wedding, yes?" the registrar posed to Zola once they made it to the altar.

"Yes!" Zola said, pulling Zena in front of herself. "But not me—her."

Zola looked at Alton and communicated the plans to him with no words.

"Wedding, yes?" the registrar looked at Adan and Zena, his new subjects, as if it made no difference to him who got married. They could even pull a pair from the crowd forward.

When Zena, who was looking at Adan, did not respond to the registrar's eye prodding, he looked at Adan and repeated, "Wedding, yes?"

"Wedding, yes!" Adan replied.

The registrar said over the clapping crowd, "Wedding, yes?"

"Yes! Wedding, yes!" Zena nodded. "Yes!"

Zena felt the way anyone does when they're next in line and plucked from a crowd to receive their heart's desire. As if luck had finally chosen her. And it felt so good. This was her wedding. Her wedding to Adan. Their wedding in Bali, on the beach, with people they loved, with people they'd never know. And it felt right.

Adan had taken both of Zena's hands.

"This is my dream. You are my dream," he said. "I let you go so many years ago. I pushed you away. But I was a boy then. Now I'm a man and I know it wasn't right. I know for sure I'm the luckiest man who ever lived if you say yes to be mine. And if you take me back, not a day will go by when it's not clear that I know that—that I'm lucky to have you. I'm never leaving again. I'm never turning away again. I'm here to stay."

Zena started her vows with the first thing that came to mind: "I shouldn't take you back!" she joked, and Alton and Zola laughed. "But I have to. I have to take you back because you're my love. You're the only man I've ever loved. That's something I've kept in secret from everyone, from you, from myself, for too long, but I'm not willing to live in secret with that anymore. I'm not willing to live without you anymore. So, Adan, I vow to hold on to you. To be open to you. To the experience of you now, as you are now. And I'm never turning away again. I'm here to stay."

"Do you take this woman to be your lawfully wedded wife?" the registrar asked Adan.

"I do."

The registrar turned to Zena and asked, "Do

you take this man to be your lawfully wedded husband?"

"I do," Zena replied, and Adan wiped his forehead nervously for a laugh from the crowd.

Adan pulled two gold bands out of his suit jacket. "I've been carrying these rings around for years. They remind me of the love I thought I lost, but now I've gotten a second chance.

Adan slid the band onto Zena's ring finger, and then she put the ring Adan had given her onto his ring finger.

They separated and looked into each other's eyes, feeling the weight of those rings on their fingers.

"I now pronounce you husband and wife," the registrar said. "And you may now kiss the bride."

Adan stepped close to Zena, pairing the tips of his shoes with hers.

"Can you believe this?" she said as he leaned down to her.

"Yes," he said.

Adan lifted Zena into the air and lowered her down to his lips.

And there, with the sun beaming behind them, Mr. and Mrs. Adan Frederick Douglass celebrated their first kiss as husband and wife.

* * * * *

REQUEST YOUR FREE BOOKS!

2 FREE NOVELS PLUS 2 FREE GIFTS!

KIMANI™ ROMANCE

Love's ultimate destination!

YES! Please send me 2 FREE Harlequin® Kimani™ Romance novels and my 2 FREE gifts (gifts are worth about $10). After receiving them, if I don't wish to receive any more books, I can return the shipping statement marked "cancel." If I don't cancel, I will receive 4 brand-new novels every month and be billed just $5.44 per book in the U.S. or $5.99 per book in Canada. That's a savings of at least 16% off the cover price. It's quite a bargain! Shipping and handling is just 50¢ per book in the U.S. and 75¢ per book in Canada.* I understand that accepting the 2 free books and gifts places me under no obligation to buy anything. I can always return a shipment and cancel at any time. Even if I never buy another book, the two free books and gifts are mine to keep forever.

168/368 XDN GH4P

Name	(PLEASE PRINT)	
Address		Apt. #
City	State/Prov.	Zip/Postal Code

Signature (if under 18, a parent or guardian must sign)

Mail to the **Reader Service:**
IN U.S.A.: P.O. Box 1867, Buffalo, NY 14240-1867
IN CANADA: P.O. Box 609, Fort Erie, Ontario L2A 5X3

Want to try two free books from another line?
Call 1-800-873-8635 or visit www.ReaderService.com.

* Terms and prices subject to change without notice. Prices do not include applicable taxes. Sales tax applicable in N.Y. Canadian residents will be charged applicable taxes. Offer not valid in Quebec. This offer is limited to one order per household. Not valid for current subscribers to Harlequin® Kimani™ Romance books. All orders subject to credit approval. Credit or debit balances in a customer's account(s) may be offset by any other outstanding balance owed by or to the customer. Please allow 4 to 6 weeks for delivery. Offer available while quantities last.

Your Privacy—The Reader Service is committed to protecting your privacy. Our Privacy Policy is available online at www.ReaderService.com or upon request from the Reader Service.

We make a portion of our mailing list available to reputable third parties that offer products we believe may interest you. If you prefer that we not exchange your name with third parties, or if you wish to clarify or modify your communication preferences, please visit us at www.ReaderService.com/consumerschoice or write to us at Reader Service Preference Service, P.O. Box 9062, Buffalo, NY 14240-9062. Include your complete name and address.

KROM15

Turn your love of reading into rewards you'll love with
Harlequin My Rewards

Join for FREE today at
www.HarlequinMyRewards.com

Earn **FREE BOOKS** of your choice.

Experience **EXCLUSIVE OFFERS** and contests.

Enjoy **BOOK RECOMMENDATIONS**
selected just for you.

PLUS! Sign up now
and get **500** points
right away!

Earn
FREE
REWARDS
HarlequinMyRewards.com
Join
Today!

MYR16R